A Myriad of Worlds of the Silver-tongued

Alina Anthony

BLUE FORGE PRESS
Port Orchard  Washington

A Myriad of Worlds of the Silver-tongued
Copyright 2024
by Alina Anthony

First eBook Edition May 2025
First Print Edition May 2025

ISBN 979-8-89439-043-7

For information about film, reprint or other subsidiary rights, contact: blueforgegroup@gmail.com

This is a work of fiction. Names, characters, locations, and all other story elements are the product of the authors' imaginations and are used fictitiously. Any resemblance to actual persons, living or dead, or other elements in real life, is purely coincidental.

Blue Forge Press is the print division of the volunteer-run, federal 501(c)3 nonprofit, Blue Legacy (EIN 83-4307421), founded in 1989 and dedicated to supporting artisans marginalized due to race, age, disability, economics or other factors. We strive to empower storytellers from all walks of life with our four divisions: Blue Forge Press, Blue Forge Films, Blue Forge Gaming, and Blue Forge Sound. Find out more at www.BlueForgeGroup.org

Blue Forge Press
7419 Ebbert Drive Southeast
Port Orchard, Washington 98367
blueforgepress@gmail.com
360-550-2071 ph.txt

Table of Contents

A Myriad of Worlds of the Silver-tongued

Alina Anthony

Emerald Eyes

It was a day like every other day. Octavia found herself sitting at her computer, watching the cursor flash on the Word document. With every flash, she thought about every previous book sale she had in the past, how easily every story came to her. Now she found her muse had left her hanging, off somewhere on vacation perhaps.

Leaning forward on her desk, sinking her face into her hands, her fingers massaging between her eyes to her forehead, Octavia let out a deep guttural sigh. "How am I going to meet my deadline?" She was speaking to no one in particular, as she sat in her office alone except for an adult bearded dragon in a large enclosure across the room from her.

Peeking at the blank page on her computer screen once more, she found herself closing the application to reveal travel plans on a web browser. The screen before her read "Elevated Travel Agency," and before Octavia realized she had booked herself a full trip to Norway. With the full intention to visit the oldest regions where the Vikings lived, this had to bring some sort of inspiration for her new book, right?

After printing off her itinerary, Octavia closed everything on her desktop computer. Having lived in a house with a father so completely obsessed with technology, he had taught her the ins and outs of choosing the right equipment for what purpose. While she used a desktop most of the time while at home to write her books, she always backed up her work to a cloud so she could take it to go with her laptop if the need arose. And this time, she was taking her work to Norway!

Backing her computer chair out from her desk, Octavia bent over and pulled a large drawer out to reveal the sleek looking laptop with the charging cable sitting on top. Removing the laptop from her desk, she stood looking for an empty outlet to charge her laptop for preparation of writing on the go. Walking across the room with the laptop tucked under her arm, she looked near the enclosure finding a powerstrip with a few empty slots available.

Glancing over at the brown and orange bearded dragon resting on a large cork log craning its head in such a way to see what she was doing, she smiled. "Hello there Ember." Standing up from plugging in her laptop, she looked over the enclosure to see the beardie had eaten most of her greens and the crickets she had given him earlier that day. "I am going to have my assistant come look after you while I am gone." As Octavia spoke to the dragon, it moved its head as if it knew what she was saying, its gold eyes watching her as it moved and tilted its arrow shaped head.

Later that evening Octavia found herself standing in the airport staring at a moving tv screen showing all the flights that were taking off that day. Every now and again the screen would refresh with updates, some flights showing delays, others appearing to be arriving much earlier than previously anticipated. Finding her flight on the board she noted the gate. "Okay, I must go to gate three."

Gripping the handle of her suitcase tightly, she found herself turning away from the screen to find the counter of the airline that would be taking her from one country to another. Sliding in line behind a tall man who had dark hair and smelled wonderful, she smiled to herself as she adjusted the straps of her carryon backpack. Pulling her itinerary out of her jacket pocket, she looked over what her seat number was. Moving up person by person, finally she had checked her bag and made it to the part where she would be getting on the plane for Norway.

Double, triple checking she had all of her identification, most importantly her passport, Octavia found herself on the plane in her seat nestled in business class. She had some perks from being a known author, and it seemed she was to be seated across from the tall man who smelled nice. Her plane partner was a small blonde woman who spoke with a soft Norwegian accent and wore a light pink business suit, who wasted no time pulling out her laptop to work.

As everyone filed on to the plane, Octavia stored her bag under her seat as instructed. Every now and again an airline attendant would walk by helping the passengers get settled in for the very long flight, and finally one came to address her plane partner to wait to turn on any electronics until they were in the air.

Watching the blonde woman store her laptop, Octavia turned to her. "Work?"

The blonde smiled at her after leaning down from storing her computer. "Yes, I am a lawyer and I have a lot of correspondence to catch up on." Octavia didn't say much after that, as her mind fell back on the work she had neglected for so long. The point of this trip wasn't just for her work—no, this was a spiritual trip. A trip meant for her to search deeper inside herself. An eat, pray, love sort of trip.

Nine hours and some change later, Octavia stood jet-lagged in the airport of Oslo, Norway, with her backpack secured to her back she stared at the belt that continuously cycled everyone's baggage around and around. Finally, her large purple suitcase appeared with the leather luggage tag that indicated it was hers, and she reached in at just that moment when she collided with the tall man with dark hair. It was then she was hit with that scent reminding her of the familiarity of the man, and she felt her cheeks burn red as she pulled her heavy bag from the conveyor belt.

"I am sorry, I should have been paying better attention!" A nervous laugh left her lips at that moment.

The tall dark haired man just smiled as he too had pulled a suitcase from the moving belt, his eyes were the greenest eyes she had ever seen. It was almost eerie, but something about them drew her in. "All is well, what more can we expect in the madness of trying to retrieve our things on this moving snake." Turning to walk away, the tall man turned and spoke his farewells to Octavia. "May your travels be safe, miss." His accent was full and thick, but that wasn't what kept her watching him.

Octavia smiled watching the man she nearly plowed over getting her luggage walk away, and it was like he carried himself in a bubble different than everyone else around him.

Feeling a light buzzing in her pocket, Octavia took her

eyes off the man for a moment to pull out her phone. Looking up as the man was no longer in sight, a puzzling look came over her as there wasn't anywhere he could have gone, no door to escape through or a place to sit for that matter. Maybe he just walks faster than she thought?

Shrugging off the thought of the man, she raised the handle of her luggage and started to drag it down the long hallway towards the counters where most people who rented cars stood in line. Finally getting the keys to her car with the briefest of interactions with the clerk, she found her way to the lot that held her car. Staring down at the keyfob that laid in the palm of her left hand, she studied the blue and white symbol before she slid the pad of her thumb over the trunk button in hopes she was close enough it would work. Pressing down hard on the button, she looked up in time to catch the trunk of a gold bmw sedan pop open, waving at her in the distance she now knew how much further it would be until she would be on the road in Norway.

With the thought of what it meant for her to be this far from home, Octavia lingered at the trunk of the bmw both hands on the top of the raised hatch. "I can do this." Her words spoken for only herself, she slammed the trunk closed wasting no time to get in the driver seat.

Leaving the parking lot meant for the rental cars at the airport was easy enough, finding her hotel with the help of the navigation feature of the car was an added bonus, a premeditated move due to her preplanning for this trip. It wasn't long until the voice over the car speakers led her straight to her hotel, where Octavia parked the car with little trouble.

The sun was dipping behind the clouds at that moment, setting in Oslo, Norway, and Octavia was extremely jetlagged. Tired was an understatement, but she was prepared to rest for the night and get straight to her plan.

She had it perfectly planned out in her head. She was going to explore her roots. Reach out to the old gods, breathe in the air that belongs to her ancestors. Part of Octavia's spiritual drive came influenced by her assistant, and personal research. Every step she took felt incredibly right to her, and if all else fails, take that spiritual walk. Right?

Sliding her card into the reader on the door, the click of the green light indicating it was time for her to turn the knob. Shouldering open her door and finding a light switch, she ditched her bag near the dresser. Slipping her arms out of the special backpack made with all the extra padding to protect her laptop, she carefully left it on the bedspread of white. Walking to the windows that looked out to the dusk covered Oslo, she stood there what seemed like forever.

Bracing herself against the window frame, she leaned in close enough to see her breath on the window. "What am I doing?" A nervous laugh left her as she pushed away from the window, moving to extract the laptop from her bag. She sat on top of the bed spread with her legs crisscrossed. "Oh right! I am on a spiritual journey in hopes that it sparks my muse, and I can get this book finished!" Holding on to the laptop still closed, she fell back landing her head on the pillows. Resting the laptop on her body, she stared up at the ceiling. Feeling the burn of exhaustion threatening to close her eyelids, Octavia turned over to lay the laptop on the nightstand. Having planned on showering before bed had gone out the window with every other thought of what she wanted to do, for the exception of one thing.

Sitting up Octavia removed her phone from her pocket to rest it near the laptop, sliding from the bed; she slipped her feet out of her tennis shoes. Turning her gaze upon the suitcase that harbored all of her clothes, she sluggishly moved to it flipping on its back like a turtle; pulling the zipper to open the lid. Mindlessly digging through all her clothing, extra shoes and other necessities, she pulled out a small statue of copper. Looking over the fine details of this altar piece, she sat it on the free night stand on the other side of her bed with other pieces she had brought with her. Saying a small prayer at the stand, Octavia disappeared into the bathroom with her toiletry bag to care for her face and pearly whites. Changing into her pajamas was the last thing on her list to complete, as looking over her itinerary took precedence over anything else. Lying back she glanced over at her makeshift altar then back to her planned list, and it wasn't long before sleep took over Octavia.

That night a dream slipped over her, something unusual unlike what she often dreamt at home.

She could smell the man with the dark hair and intense green eyes, the smell of his cologne lingered on the air as she walked through the thick wet grass down to the water's edge. A thick fog was rolling in from the cold water, a deep silence came over the area around her. Something was rolling in the water, it was large and dark. It was hard for her to really make out what she was seeing in the water, it was too large to be a fish; could it be a whale? The way the water rippled against the bank was different than if any school of fish or whale were nearby or so she convinced herself; it was much like the disturbance of boats on the water. Moving closer to the water's edge to look out, she felt something slide up against her leg in the tall grass as the sound of splashing water came up from the bank. It wrapped itself around her once, twice and pulled her, and then it was gone.

Waking in a cool sweat, Octavia moved to the desk that every hotel room came standard with. Pulling out her notebook, she started writing down notes. It had become a habit of hers to write down her dreams, even the ones that tend to be on the creepy side. Her eyes followed her quick scratchings of "Fog, dark waters, ripples," and the like, all in the hopes that this would lead to a new book. Dropping the pen where it stood after a few lines of chicken scratch, she wiped her arm across her forehead pulling the moisture away from her forehead. Lingering on the thoughts of her dream or was it a nightmare? Either way, one thing was for sure Octavia had a long road ahead of her both spiritually and physically when it came to getting her deadline met. Checking the time, the alarm clock read seven o'clock in the morning—far too early, she thought. Shrugging away her thoughts, and a hot shower later, Octavia found herself on the roads of Norway once more not with books in mind but with her spirituality and connecting to the otherside.

Fiddling with the navigation while she drove, making sure she had punched in the town in which she wanted to visit for the day correctly, her eyes ducked down below the steering wheel a moment granting her a horn blow or two.

Not realizing she had swerved a few times, she felt the heat of embarrassment rise upon her cheeks as she gripped the steering wheel tighter as if it would keep her from distracting herself even more.

"Come on Octavia, you have to focus." Nothing like a little pep talk to keep her going, she thought. Tonsberg was only sixty miles from Oslo, at least that is what all the directions she googled the night before had told her. Finally the lady's voice came over the speaker telling her to take the exit needed to dump herself off in the coastal town of Tonsberg, a feeling of relief came over her. "Finally!"

Tonsberg was known as the oldest city with an unmatched Viking history, and this just sparked further obsession with her heritage but more with her new spirituality with the Norse pantheon. Driving through the city, most of the houses faced the sea. It was truly a sight to behold, Octavia thought, to touch the same earth her ancestors touched. Earlier that day she had booked herself a voyage on the archaeologically accurate Viking ship the Saga Oseberg, a must do according to anyone else who were so lucky to find themselves experiencing what the Vikings experienced on this type of a ship. With the help of the good old navigation once more, Octavia parked her rental near the docks where this long wooden magnificent scene from History's "Vikings" stood afloat the cold dark waters.

Standing with the backseat door open pulling out her jacket, she stood to stare out at the ship moving up and down on the waters.

"Beautiful, isn't she?" A man's voice broke the silence that Octavia stood in, the odd peace that she basked in while imagining what it was like to sail across the seas on a ship such as the Saga Oseberg.

Meeting the dark gray gaze of the man, she smiled. "Oh yes it is!" Closing the door of her rental car, she found the button on the fob she clutched tightly in her right hand; locking the doors.

The man who spoke to her sported graying hair, a stout build and stubble on his chin, his smile was reassuring. "Forgive me, my name is Jon, I am going to be the instructor and guide on this fun Viking excursion." Offering his hand to Octavia with a gentle smile, she placed her hand in his.

"Excuse my rudeness, I am Octavia. Nice to meet you." She watched the man look about, noticing the crowd growing near the ship, and broke the handshake. "Please excuse me, it is time to explain the rules and how to handle this beast on the waters," he told her.

Walking away to greet the other rowers of the boat, Octavia watched a moment longer before joining the rest of the lucky few who too would become a Viking that day, rowing around in the bay outside of Tonsberg.

Each of the passengers had been fully equipped with the proper safety gear, for that "just in case" moment. Tugging on the straps of her life jacket, Octavia had been assigned a place on the boat near the front on the outside, her rowing partner was a big burly looking man who appeared to be in his late forties and balding. He grinned across the way to others that appeared to be a part of a group, speaking in what she thought to be German they laughed while she felt awkward awaiting for further instructions as Jon prepared them for their departure. Given the okay, Jon stood at the front of the ship barking orders. "Row!" Everyone in unison began to row the boat from its resting place at the pier, and they soon found they were building up momentum. It was quite the sight, the feeling of the boat bouncing on the waves of the water below them made her nervous. Often Octavia glanced at her rowing partner who occasionally grinned at her, then turned his attention back to Jon or his companions. After some time they were ordered to stop, and Jon would go over the history of boat makers and the tools that were used to make this boat. It was all very fascinating,

After having spent a few hours out on the ocean in a Viking boat, Octavia could tell her assistant that she helped successfully dock a Viking ship. Sliding her phone away in her pocket after getting a picture of herself and the crew who all rowed during their trip out to sea, she said her goodbyes to the instructor and everyone else.

Before she left the dock she caught sight of something large rolling out in the sea, something that seemed too large to be a whale. Squinting her eyes, she tried hard to see what it could be. Further away she saw something else rise up and then plunge back in. It appeared to be the same thing she had been looking at but in a different place at the same time? Shaking her head a moment, Octavia laughed rubbing her sore arms. "I have to be exhausted. And just seeing things."

Turning away to walk to her car, she caught the scent of the man with dark hair. Stopping midstep, she looked around but the man from the airport was nowhere to be seen. "I need to get back to Oslo, I think rowing took it out of me." Getting back into her car, she pushed the button that started her car. Leaving the town of Tonsberg was much simpler than she anticipated, the highway taking her from the first Viking city ran along the water's edge this time, which seemed odd. Regardless of the scenery on the way back to Oslo, Octavia found herself clenching her fingers tightly around the steering wheel. Leaning forward her eyes feeling absolutely tired, her arms burning from rowing that afternoon; pep talking herself. "You can make this sixty mile drive back to your hotel room, to that big fluffy bed. Yes."

Closing her eyes for that moment, she could smell saltwater. Did she open her window? It had been a split second to Octavia, a blink and the road was near the water. The ocean itself was closer than before, and she could smell the salt on the air through the vents of her rental vehicle. Glancing down at the navigation screen it read correctly, her headlights were on showing the line dotted road ahead of her. "Hm, everything seems right." Looking out her own window she realized she hadn't seen another driver in several miles, and it almost felt like the road was moving itself. Feeling a bit disoriented, Octavia felt it was best to find a gas station or a truck stop to take a short stop at. As she continued her journey following the voices instructions on the navigation, her eyes kept drifting from the road to the ocean that now appeared to be at the roadside. The waters were dark in contrast to the sky as the sun had begun to set, and the waves were crashing hard against the barrier near the roadway.

The lines of the road started to blur in the lighting of her headlights, they almost started to melt into the asphalt taking on a more shimmering sheen. Blinking a few more times she thought she noticed the ground she drove on ahead had a design etched into it, but then she caught sight of a sign on the right side of the road notifying her of a gas station coming up at the next exit. Looking back at the road again the dotted lines that separated the two sides of the road were where they were supposed to be, leaving Octavia blinking her eyes hard a few times testing her sleepiness levels.

"I can't be that tired, can I? I mean rowing, maybe the sun took it out of me." Rolling her shoulders a few times while keeping her hands on the wheel, she saw the exit for the gas station and lowered her speed to take what was considered an exit. Taking the short road off the right of the road spilling her into a small gas station, the lights were on and it appeared to be occupied by another driver. This man leaned over an open hood, a dirty rag in hand he tinkered with something under the hood as she pulled in next to him.

Exiting the vehicle took no time for her. Octavia didn't want to linger too long at the gas station, especially if she was as tired as she assumed she was. Walking past the man who was bent over the car she felt a soft breeze touch her hair, leaving a familiar scent behind. Glancing at the man who had blonde hair tied back in a long ponytail, she shook her head while pulling the glass door of the convenience store.

Stepping into the store she was quickly greeted by a young woman who had a very muscle filled dog at her side who wore a vest that read "Emotional Support Dog," and this dog was unlike any dog Octavia had ever seen before.

"Hello there! Is there anything I can help you find?" The smile beamed on the young woman's face, her eyes never leaving Octavia for a moment. "Coffee?" Moving around the rather large dog, the woman walked Octavia around a few aisles to a coffee bar. "Fresh brewed."

Returning the smile, Octavia reached for their medium size, determining that it would be enough to get her back and not too much to keep her up all night. Her reasoning was a bit off, but she was having the most bizarre ride back to Oslo.

Octavia paid for her drink without any other troubles, except her eyes kept drifting down to the young woman's service dog. She couldn't quite place the breed of this dog, but didn't want to be rude and ask any questions. Exiting the gas station, she saw the man sitting on the curb near his car. "Car trouble?"

Why didn't she just keep her mouth shut?

"The man looked up with the most body piercing gaze, green eyes so unusual that they stood out against his complexion. Oddly familiar, she was startled at first. That scent again. "Yes, it happens every now and again. Tricky machinery."

Octavia had made her way to the driver's side of her car. Reaching down to open the door, she looked up and the man was gone.

Looking around, the door of the gas station was still. Did she miss him getting up and entering the gas station? Quickly sliding into the driver's seat, Octavia shut the door and took a large gulp of the hot coffee, burning her tongue. Leaving the gas station behind, she pulled out onto the highway with a bump. Confused by the sudden bump on the road, she felt the car... shudder? Or...?

With both of her hands on the steering wheel she pulled herself closer to look out the windshield at the road. The lines were not there again—it looked like scales were carved into the road and they moved with the sudden feel of her vehicle.

"What the—?!" Looking outside the driver's side window to see water right next to the road, now she was truly doubting that this was the right road back to Oslo.

"What is this? A snake? Oh come on, Octavia! That is silly." Now she spoke out loud to herself as she drove, leaning down she initiated the navigation.

The woman's voice came over the speakers telling her to continue down the current highway, which at this point seemed wrong. Was it the jet lag? Sleep deprivation? Octavia pined over every little thought in her head as to why this same route back to Oslo seemed completely different, and for obvious reasons many of her answers didn't make sense.

Suddenly it was right there, that dog she had seen at the gas station! Slamming on her breaks, she felt the tires of the car struggling to stop on the surface of the road. The dog looked at her through the windshield as she gasped for air, then howled an eerie howl unlike anything she heard and ran to the left disappearing into a fog that now rolled in from the water's edge.

Still grasping the steering wheel as if it was her life line, she peeled her fingers free allowing herself to put the car in park. Checking her rearview mirror, it was clear there was no one else on this highway and that was truly a scary thought. Rolling the window down to let in the night air, she felt as if this would help her catch the breath she lost in the moment of stopping in emergency mode.

Putting the car into park Octavia let herself out of the car, and stepped over to the barrier between her and the water. Looking over the water, she felt incredibly overwhelmed with everything that was happening and all it did was leave her questioning so much more of her beliefs.

It was then the very road she stood upon started to vibrate almost, moving under her so unusually it was clear that it wasn't an actual earthquake. The smell of the water around her became stronger as the ground under her rose up and suddenly slammed down, sending waves of ocean water to wash over her. Screaming, she ran to where her car stood and grabbing onto the open car door, she could see the dark mass of the road arching up and rolling, moving her car out and away from her. Ice water continued to rain down upon her as she lost her grip on the car door, and falling onto her left side she felt the ground under her hands, which felt like a snake's skin. It was then she remembered some of her reading about the world serpent and it was with that last thought when Octavia fell into the dark depths of the ocean water.

A familiar voice yelled orders to others around him, each of them acting accordingly to what they were told to do. Each and every one of them doing the job that was given to them, white lights flooded the area giving off a warmth.

It was then Octavia could smell that cologne again, her eyes opening to the dark haired man above her, his vibrant green eyes shining with a softness as he welcomed her back to the land of the living. "Welcome back! Please don't attempt to move or sit up. You've been in a terrible accident."

Blinking once, then twice, she coughed several times. The taste of salt water rose up in her throat, sending her over onto her side to throw up water. Reaching up to touch her mouth, she saw cuts on her arms.

The man's familiar voice spoke once more, finally bringing her attention back. Her mind was still so foggy, she coughed a few more times allowing the water to rise up and out of her body. "Please, just lie back, Octavia, we are going to transport you to the hospital in Oslo."

Trying to speak, her throat was dry from all the salt, but she couldn't look away from him.

"My name is Luka, we met at the airport two days ago."

How could she forget that smell, and those eyes? She had never seen anyone with eyes like those before, except when. "How? How did I?"

Luka was quick to answer. "It appears you took an old route back to Oslo. It led you to a bridge near the ocean that was out and you took a plunge."

Of course that isn't how she remembered it. No, it wasn't a bridge.

It was a serpent and he was there.

Book of Shadows

It was just like any other day at Remington's Book Cellar. The old man had a new batch of books that were on the bestseller's list come in, and, as always, he left the work for him to complete. Alaric found himself spending his Saturdays working for old man Remington, unloading boxes of books to carts, helping Amelia label them with the proper price, and, if time allowed, he would help with the displays.

See, Remington had been around for a long time; he was known as one of the only local book dealers left in the area. Alaric found a love for books as a young boy, thanks to his mother painting the worlds with her words for him, inspiring him to read more than watch movies. On one special Saturday, his mother took him to Remington's Book Cellar to pick out a new book, and his love for this small-looking shop on the outside, but large pile of books on the inside, grew.

Alaric had entered through the back storeroom to find boxes of books lying in wait, as if begging him to pick them up. Amelia came rushing by with a handful of price points and a label gun, her face looking flustered, and her messy bun seeming messier than usual.

"Busy day already, Amelia?"

Alaric moved out of her way as she passed by in a huff, her eyes glancing at him through wire gold frames. "Alaric! You have no idea! Mr. Remington ordered too much again! This time, he brought in some rare books with the new ones, and I am having to rush around looking for his research." Pausing to catch her breath, she stopped to look at Alaric as he bent down to pick up a box that had an odd-looking label.

"There are more further in the back, and I think Mr. Remington wants you to take the rare books and put them in the lock case. Something about some potential buyers coming to view them next week?"

Shrugging her shoulders, she found herself losing some of the price points. Kneeling down to grab the paper, she stood and disappeared without waiting for an answer from Alaric.

It was quite common for Amelia to spout off a lot of information and suddenly disappear to do something else; she liked to call it "multitasking."

Looking at the box in his hands, Alaric walked back to a workbench that held a few other boxes that lay open. Peeking inside, the boxes were some of the newest books that were being displayed in the front window. Locating an empty cart, Alaric finished emptying the boxes onto the cart.

After breaking down and putting the boxes into a neat pile near the bench, Alaric went to work unloading other open boxes that Amelia had opened to verify that the books that were ordered had indeed come. Alaric hated how disorganized everything always was when he came in on Saturdays, but after the first two hours of organizing and unloading already opened boxes, he soon found the boxes that held some of the rarer books.

Kneeling down to stack some of the boxes, he spied a box that appeared to have been ripped open.

"That's odd."

Picking up the stack of boxes, he heard Amelia come into the back room.

"What's odd, Alaric?"

She always had great timing. Turning to set the two boxes on the countertop, he looked at the dark-haired girl.

"One of the boxes of rare books appears to be ripped open."

Starting to kneel down to investigate further, Amelia made a quizzical look as she moved to take the cart he had just filled.

"That is odd. Maybe it ripped when the delivery guy brought it in? I hope none of the books were damaged."

Walking away with the cart of books, Alaric followed her with his blue eyes, brows raised. The odd thing about this box was it was under the workbench; it looked like something had torn its way out of the box.

Returning to his feet with the box in his hands, he looked over the box, finding a weird-looking label. Unable to read where the box came from, Alaric knelt down again, dragging his hands under the workbench that was dark now.

It was as if a shadow had filled the area he was dragging his hands in. Searching for books, or even a lost invoice, Alaric felt a sharp stab over the top of his hand so quick, he jolted backward onto his butt.

Holding his hand, Alaric examined the top of his right hand, spotting two small spots of blood. Wiping at the small wounds on his hand, it almost appeared like a cat's claw had gotten hooked in his flesh the moment he felt the stab.

Rubbing his left hand over the right a couple of times, he then leaned over to look under the workbench again out of curiosity. Was there a cat in the bookshop?

Now placing his hands flat on the dense carpeting, he leaned his face close to the ground to peer under. His eyes could now see under the workbench; it appeared the overhead lighting now reached underneath again.

"How strange."

Sitting up, Alaric pondered what happened to him as he looked for anything that may have come out of the empty box. Shaking his head slightly, he maneuvered himself in a way that made it easier for him to stand up.

Later that day, after everything was unloaded and put away as needed, Alaric went back to the box that lay upon the workbench. Looking at it closer, he thought he saw claw marks from the inside of the box, but it seemed impossible.

Looking away, he saw Amelia shouting from the doorway leading into the backroom.

"What?" Alaric replied.

"I am taking off. Mr. Remington is pleased with our work and said we could leave when we finished cleaning up. So, when you've finished the backroom, you're clear to leave."

Smiling, she turned and left without hearing a reply from Alaric. It was typical of Amelia to do that to him; he was pretty used to her doing that.

Nodding his reply to an empty room, he went back to looking at the box. The marks were no longer there. Shocked by what he no longer saw, he picked up the box, opening and closing the flaps, looking for the claw marks that no longer appeared.

Perplexed by what he saw, Alaric took to finishing the cleaning of the backroom. Taking all the boxes but the one he found perplexing out to the back dumpster, Alaric took this one box and left it in a spot on the shelf with a note taped to the side that stated, "Save!!"

Taking the supplies he had used to hang the posters to the backroom, he noticed the case that held the rare finds had a reflection.

"A cat?"

Turning behind him to see the black cat—only there was nothing. Looking at the case once again, he felt his eyes widen.

"Am I going crazy?"

Looking around the bookcase he saw the cat in front of, and around other displays, he couldn't find any trace of the cat he saw in the glass display case.

Looking up, Mr. Remington waved at Alaric.

"Did you finish with the posters?"

Glancing over at the case once more, then back to Mr. Remington. "Yes, sir!"

Eyeing Alaric for a moment, the old man smiled.

"Well, could you check the lighting in the back corner of the shop? It seems darker. I wonder if one of the bulbs burnt out?"

"Sure, sure," Alaric said. Turning, he continued on his mission to put his supplies away and to fetch a step ladder to inspect the lighting back in the mystery section of the bookstore.

The mystery section of the store had always held a bit of a darker side with some of the writers they carried there, but the very back corner seemed black. Setting out the step ladder, Alaric looked up at the light housing. Everything appeared to be working just fine. A few times the bulbs in the double fixture would flicker, but that was something that always happened with that fixture.

Climbing the ladder, Alaric unscrewed the knob that held the saucer plate to the electrical portion of the piece, examining the bulbs carefully. Tapping the side of the electrical portions of the housing, with nothing happening, he quickly replaced the ornate glass piece so that he could descend the ladder.

"Strange."

Even though the lighting appeared to be working just fine in the corner of the store, it still seemed darker than the rest of the store.

Shaking his head, Alaric packed everything up and moved to his cleaning duties. For the rest of the day, it seemed there was a lingering darkness that sat in the back corner of the store, and, as customers came and went, some visited that corner.

Weeks had gone by, and the corner in the back of the store continued to stay dark. In fact, it appeared to get darker and darker. Every now and again, Alaric caught the glimpse of cat eyes in the reflection of the glass case that held the rare books, but he could never figure out where this cat was.

Mr. Remington brought more and more posters to

decorate the front window by the double wood doors that entered the book cellar, each one holding the picture of a man or woman who had gone missing. Some days, they had family members of some of those folks coming in, looking around the bookshop—many of them upset, almost insane with sadness—trying to find the answers to why their loved one suddenly went missing.

At one point, they had to close the shop due to one of the missing person's family members getting violent, throwing books from shelves as if there was some secret doorway that led them to where they were being kept. It was truly a sad sight for everyone involved.

Alaric kept to his daily duties every Saturday, and finally, he noticed black paw prints leading from the back corner of the shop. Curiosity crept in as he followed these soot-looking markings. Kneeling down, reaching out to touch the spot, they faded like a shadow being overtaken by light.

Looking up from where he had followed the paw prints, he found a book opened, stuck between the bookshelves. It appeared to be a very old book. The binding was well worn and made of a different material than most of the old books that Mr. Remington brought in.

Reaching in between the shelving units, he caught a sharp twinge feeling as he pulled the book free. Two blood welts appeared on his hand.

"Again?"

Holding the book in one hand, he shook the one that just took on cat claw marks. Bringing the welts to his mouth to suck the blood that was forming on the top of his skin, he eyed the odd-looking book. Something about the way the binding felt in his hand was different than most books. This one felt harder than usual.

The leather of the book was different. Opening to the front page, words were written in a foreign language that were curved and delicately etched inside. Holding the book open, Alaric felt the uncontrollable urge to trace the letters of the page.

Flipping through the pages of the book carefully, he caught a glimpse of fur. In the middle of the book, marked by a sewn-in marker, it appeared to have been fashioned out of a cat's tail.

"You've got to be *kidding* me!"

Closing the book in a hurry, he stood to take the book to the rarities counter. On his heels, he felt a heaviness.

Stepping in behind the counter to find the keys that Mr. Remington kept hidden in the drawer, Alaric carefully placed the worn black leather book in the glass display case. With the storing of the book came a bit of a lighter feeling in the shop, but never any answers to what happened to each of the shoppers that came to visit the Book Cellar.

Some rumors came from the darkness that sat in the back corner of the mystery section that if you saw a black cat with green eyes—steer clear. That the cat was a gatekeeper of another world.

People disappeared every now and again since the mysterious book found its place in the bookcase, always following the glimpse of a black cat. The box in the backroom continued to be a mystery to the young man, as he studied the black book now locked away in the glass case.

ater that month, Mr. Remington met Alaric in the closing hours of a Saturday with the mysterious black book in hand. Alaric's eyes widened as he watched the old man finger through the light feather paper of the book, his fingers finding the interesting choice of a bookmark.

"Alaric? Where did you find this book?"

Still watching as the bookseller's hands moved delicately over the bookbinding, studying the material, he swallowed slowly. "I found it wedged between two of the shelves in the back corner of the mystery section..."

Hearing Mr. Remington hum an answer in acknowledgement, Alaric's eyes met two small green orbs that hovered near the mystery section, where a large black mist was starting to form. It was like a fog of black had flowed in through the back of the bookstore to fill in the space before the bookshelves, creating an endless void ready to devour everything that came into contact with it.

"I think that, um, it would be best to—"

Looking up, Mr. Remington waited for Alaric to finish his sentence before his gray eyes hardened a moment, then softened with a smile.

Closing the book with a harsh slap, he pushed the book into the boy's hands.

"Here, put this away, please. Make sure to lock the case and the store. You did great, as always. See you next Saturday!"

With that, the old man made quite a quick exit, leaving behind a boy with a book and a void to be filled.

Firestorm

There they were, standing so tall, the dark rough patches of bark growing up and up. The smell of them, as the water had cascaded down their tall statures the night before, graced the underbrush with a soft caress, giving life essence to everything that lived beneath their massive canopies. The trees were beautiful and wise, each one growing larger than the next—some carrying battle scars from natural wars fought across the land.

It is taught to us to treasure these large timbers, to give thanks for everything they bring us: shelter, food, and much, much more.

Reaching down and taking a fistful of earth, she brought it to her nose and took a deep breath. Closing her eyes, Eden could see the earthworms moving through the soil, devouring the decay with the promise of returning it as new earth. Sprinkling the soil back where she had scooped it from, she knelt closer and whispered softly to it.

With that, she stood beneath the large trees. Looking up, she could only guess at the ages of these towering giants. Smiling, she spun in a circle, the sleeves of her winged sweater catching the breeze. Feeling the snapping and crunching of wet leaves and twigs beneath her boots, she felt utter bliss in that very moment.

Who could possibly ever leave this place?

Deep inside the oldest part of the forest stood a small cottage that appeared to have stood against time itself, the chimney stack giving off the soft smoke of a fire burning inside. The outside of the cottage was built from both cobblestone and wood—much of it looked like it was from the fifteenth century. To strangers, the appearance of this place might seem like the beginning of many fairy tales, but to Eden, this was her place of pure tranquility. Her escape from what plagued most of human civilization: big cities and forty to sixty-hour work weeks.

Very few people were ever brought to this cottage—a staple home to her ancestors, protected and passed down through generations. With Eden being the youngest of the Reynard family, her grandmother had personally overseen her training, most importantly showing her how to protect the very dwelling that had safeguarded their lineage through history's trials and tribulations.

The cottage itself appeared to be nothing significant at first glance. But when stepping through the front door— worlds collided.

Much of history was preserved in how it was originally built, but the amenities inside were constantly upgraded to keep with the changing times. Portraits of ancestors decorated the walls, alongside built-in libraries of old books and framed maps too delicate to be touched by modern hands. The place was any archaeologist's dream, and Eden— who studied history outside her family's traditions—believed this gave her the upper hand in knowledge. In these times, it most certainly did.

At the large carved table that could fit a whole platoon sat Eden's grandmother, Rose. She was an older woman of nearly seventy-three, but her face didn't show it. Finding her with her typical cup of tea, Eden smiled just inside the door of the cottage, pulling her fingers free of leather gloves.

"Grandmother, is that jasmine tea I smell?"

Wasting no time on an answer, Eden seated herself beside the older woman, who wore her long silver hair tied in a tight round bun at the top of her head. Piercing blue eyes watched as young hands reached for the teapot, pouring water into a matching cup from a set that had obviously been around longer than Eden had breathed air.

"Why, help yourself, Eden." Rose held a faint smile as she brought her own cup to her pink-painted lips.

"Thanks, Grandmother."

The older woman watched her granddaughter with wise eyes, following her hands as Eden went through the motions of preparing her jasmine tea. "You know, if you do it right, the tea leaves may leave you answers to your questions."

Eden's movement paused. Instead of placing the leaves directly into her cup, she used an infuser. "Not today, Grandmother."

With her denial of potential answers from the universe, Eden watched as the hot water drew flavors from the tea leaves in her cup.

"You know, Eden, sometimes we can't ignore the messages the universe is trying to tell us."

Pushing herself up from the table, Rose took her tea cup away to disappear into another room of the ancient house.

Truth be told, Eden hadn't visited the Reynard cottage in many years, always giving the excuse of work. Her family found that the further she delved into her career, the less time she spent with them. And the less time she spent with family, the more she forgot who they were—and what they were meant for.

Weekly calls to Eden's mother always ended in a minor argument about how she needed to take some time off. Her papers could wait; family could not.

Even her home life was taking a hit—and her love life had already suffered. Finally, Eden gave in to her boss's request to take a vacation and visit home. In all actuality, she had the holidays off, and something inside her had pushed her to return. Living in an illusion built around working long hours to create a "good life" and provide for others had drained her—and she didn't even realize it.

Stirring the infuser full of tea, Eden sat alone, thinking about the professorship she was trying for. Everything she was doing to get it seemed to end in disaster, even though she had been given warning signs to stop.

Pulling the infuser from the cup, she inhaled the strong scent of jasmine before drinking the cooling liquid in two whole gulps. Rose would be appalled by her tea-drinking habits, but Eden knew the universe was playing a wild hand in her life.

"Why can't I just get the break I need?!"

Her words echoed in an empty room. She stood from

her seat at the table, staring down at the painted cup. The infuser sitting on the saucer popped open, spilling the clumped-up leaves in a strange design. An unusual sensation fell over Eden.

Noticing the movement on the table, she eyed the spilled leaves. "What is this..." Her voice was soft, almost full of wonder.

Placing both hands on the edge of the table to brace herself, she leaned in closer, as if to hear a message the tea leaves might whisper. Letting out a deep sigh, denying what she was seeing, Eden left the kitchen and headed to her room at the back of the cottage.

"I know my teachings," she muttered. "But in this modern world, things are much different."

Eden often spoke aloud to no one in pure frustration—although she was being heard more often than she realized.

That night, Eden retired to her room and glimpsed her reflection in the windowpane—a red fox. Just for a split second. She looked away, then back, only to see herself again: long gray sweater, black boots, the same clothes she had worn all day. How could she dismiss it so easily?

But for someone with deep family roots like hers, the disconnection was easier than one might expect. She had lost sight of it all in the blur of modern American city life.

That night, as Eden slept, she dreamt of autumn-colored leaves falling all around her like fire embers. Each leaf looked carefully carved, as if shaped by a cookie cutter. Reds, yellows, and oranges glowed with more vibrancy than any colors she'd ever dreamed before.

Tossing in her bed, she dreamt of tall, thick trees growing higher than any skyscraper, their branches reaching toward the universe. The sweet smell of decaying leaves touched her nose, and the soft squish of soil between her toes made her smile.

The sense of freedom overwhelmed her—the way she could move through the overgrowth without worry.

Then she heard it. Then she smelled it.

Fire.

Waking with a jolt, Eden sat upright, blinking and inhaling deeply through her nose, hoping it had all been a dream. It was odd—but not totally rare—for her to dream smells.

Taking a few more deep breaths, she closed her eyes, as if that would help her smell more clearly. She had to make sure the house wasn't on fire.

Flopping back onto the bed, she sighed in relief. It was the sixth time that week she'd had that dream. Not a nightmare, exactly—but something about it was different than other dreams.

Rolling onto her left side, she sat up and placed her feet on the cool wood floor. "Why do I keep having this dream..."

Watching strands of red hair fall into her face, she analyzed the color in the morning light that streamed through the curtain gaps. Hearing the sound of tires on the dirt road outside the house, Eden rose and walked to the front window.

"Well, it's just me left in this old cottage..."

She had known her grandmother would be gone for some time, as she often was, taking care of long-distance errands. Staying alone in such an old cottage, so far from civilization, could be unsettling—but Eden had grown used to Rose's disappearances.

With her grandmother gone, Eden took a long, hot shower and eventually settled at the large dining table with a hot cup of coffee. Staring into the black liquid, she saw her own eyes reflected back at her.

Tapping her fingernails against the mug, she turned toward the laptop resting idle on the tabletop. Wiggling the wireless mouse, she opened files and began to scroll through itemized lots for work. Window after window, program after program—time slipped away.

One cup of coffee turned into a whole pot.

Looking up at the hand-carved clock above the fireplace, she saw it was five-thirty in the afternoon. Her stomach growled in protest—a deep rumble that would put any animal to shame.

"I can't believe I worked all day…"

To those who knew her, this wasn't surprising. Eden had a way of getting completely lost in her work. Even now, while supposedly on holiday, she ignored the world and dove headfirst into her responsibilities.

"Guess I should make myself something to eat."

Snapping her laptop shut, she left the table and rummaged through the refrigerator. Finding leftovers from the night before, she glanced out the kitchen door toward the gravel drive where her grandmother's car would normally be parked.

"Hm… Wonder where Grandmother is…"

Cradling a sealed container of homemade pasta bake,

she returned to the counter and dished up a plate to warm in the microwave. She often worked and ate at the same time, brushing off the quiet nagging in the back of her mind.

See, humans have a way of sensing things—of knowing something before it happens. Many call it intuition or a gut instinct.

Eden felt it too.

She just ignored it that night, telling herself she was bored. That excuse gave her permission to keep working late into the evening before finally retiring to her room.

The next morning came with an odd smell. It was faint, but it was there. Eden had awoken to what appeared to be a cloudy day from the windows of the cottage, although just a glance wasn't enough to certify her as a weatherman.

With breakfast out of the way, she found herself tapping at the hollow plastic buttons of her laptop once more. Rose hadn't returned from the errands she spoke of the day before. The town was a few hours away, but it never took her this long.

"I know Grandmother said a day for her tasks, but..."

And there it was again—that smell. What was that smell?

Standing from her favored spot at the long carved table, Eden closed her eyes, concentrating on the scent that now permeated through the house. It smelled like something was on fire. That nagging feeling she had been ignoring in her stomach suddenly felt like a raging gut ache. Something was very, terribly wrong.

Running to the door that led out to the drive, Eden threw it open. What she thought had been a cloudy sky was actually heavy, thick smoke.

Stepping outside, she could smell it much more profoundly—the smell of burning trees, and something else. Turning her back to the outdoors, Eden focused her hope on the electronic device she had brought from work. Checking the internet for news, she used her cell phone as a hotspot—but something was wrong.

Clicking once, then twice on the icon for the web, she kept getting a "no connection" message.

"I know I paid my bills before I left home…"

Desperately pulling her phone from her jeans pocket, she noticed she had no service—and a warning notification about a flash fire in the area. Sliding her thumb up and down the screen, she was in shock at all the messages that had come in that morning while she'd slept through her work-induced exhaustion.

"I am going to be trapped…"

Gliding her fingers over the device, attempting to make a call, all Eden could hear was the dull tone that came when out of service range. Hoping it was just a mistake—or maybe her mother hadn't paid the phone bill—Eden tried to call her grandmother Rose. The same dead tone greeted her.

Frustration and fear began to rise. She tossed the phone onto the table near the computer—the very device that was supposed to stay behind at work.

By now, the cottage reeked of smoke. The fire was close. Racing to the kitchen door, Eden opened it. The sky was darker, the smoke a menacing beast.

"I can't believe this is happening!"

Her voice was high, trembling with fear. Her heart pounded so hard she could feel it in her throat.

CRACK!

The sound of trees splitting and falling under the heat of the flames grew louder. The monstrous firestorm was raging across the ancient forest that had protected their family home for generations.

A droplet of sweat ran from her forehead down her nose. The heat inside the cottage was rising. It felt suffocating. Eden stood just outside the kitchen door, trying to breathe—but even a shallow inhale brought on a coughing fit.

She returned to the kitchen and found a towel, soaked it in cold water, and tied it around her mouth. It would help her breathe as she stood in the firestorm, contemplating her next move.

Eden left the safety of the house for the outdoors, believing she might get better air. Looking around her, she could see the tops of massive trees collapsing under the teeth of the fire-filled monster.

Tears streaked down her now soot-covered face. This was it. This was her last day on the mortal plane.

How could I have ignored my intuition this long? The questions spiraled in her mind. What if she had left earlier? What if she had listened?

The sound of cracking, splintering trees was all around her. The fire was coming closer. Then Eden noticed something strange about the cottage.

The door had closed behind her—and shimmered, as if protected by an invisible shield.

With the towel pressed close to her face, her eyes widened. She remembered the tale passed down from her childhood—of a spell cast upon the house by her grandmother's ancestors. Women persecuted for their gifts. Women who had protected this one safe place for generations.

Hope surged in her chest.

Running toward the door, she reached for the handle—locked.

Shaking and jiggling the knob as hard as she could, Eden screamed. The heat of the flames was creeping closer, devouring the forest floor.

"Let me in!"

Tears streamed down her face. She choked on the dry air around her, coughing again and again as she screamed.

"Please! Please!"

Backing away from the door, she looked to the windows. In one of them, just for a moment, she saw someone. It looked like her grandmother Rose.

Silence.

"Help me, please!"

Desperation overtook her. Eden tried to break a window—but her force met a magical shield. She drove her elbow into the glass and was met with a shockwave of energy that flung her three feet back.

Landing on her stomach, arms outstretched, she coughed. "No! No! This can't be. I am a Reynard Witch!"

Then something happened.

The firestorm was upon her, devouring everything around the cottage that wasn't protected.

At first, she felt the burning. The way the flesh peeled under the heat. The smell of it. Her heart raced, and the adrenaline took far too long to numb the pain. She screamed.

She turned onto her back and watched ember-covered leaves fall onto her body—but they no longer burned. She couldn't smell burning flesh. She couldn't feel anything.

The sound of her heartbeat faded. Then—everything went black.

Staring up at a canopy of changing leaves—red, gold, green—black eyes blinked with wonder.

The smell of the earth gave way to a new beginning by shedding the old, leaving room for those who would frolic in the wildness of creation and the changing season.

Eden turned her eyes from the leaves to the sound of snapping twigs. Startled, she bolted and hid.

Sunlight broke through the young trees, warming the red and brown fur of the fox crouched in the brush.

Rose walked with other members of the Reynard family, carrying bags of seeds. One by one, they cast the seeds into the air. They knew Eden hadn't perished in the great firestorm.

No—she had been given a chance. A chance to live. A chance to learn what it means to listen to her instincts. To her intuition.

When the universe tells her to run, she will run.

When it is time to rest, she will rest.

Ghost Tears

And I would like to say that is how you properly investigate a haunted place!"

Shaun popped out of view of the camera, allowing his co-hosts, Dani and Jesse, to be seen by the camera they had set up earlier in the foyer of the house they were investigating earlier in the night.

"You got that right, Shaun!" Dani retorted as she hopped up on one leg then the other, her long dark hair bouncing in the high ponytail on the top of her head; her hazel eyes popping with the black and white eyeliner so expertly lining them.

Completing the trio that made up the "3 Ghost'A'Teers" was Jesse, a dark-haired male who embodied the gothic athletic aesthetic the young girls craved in their generation. Sliding in, he winked at the camera, pointing at their audience.

"Until next time, scare you later!"

Out of view of the camera, Shaun turned it off after Jesse gave his ending cue, pulling the piece of equipment off of the stand—careful to ensure none of the footage they shot on that camera was lost. Looking it over, Shaun walked over to an open case lined in foam and carefully placed the camera away with others like it.

Each of the three members of the YouTube channel 3 Ghost'A'Teers moved about the room securing their ghost hunting equipment, laughing and making snide jokes about parts of their night spent in the house-turned-art gallery.

Dani picked up two of the black cases, ready to take them out to the SUV they drove to the building together in. She yawned loudly.

"Guys! I am going to start taking out the packed equipment, and I am ready to head back to the hotel. I am dead."

Jesse, who finished his rounds of the last few rooms of the house they had last investigated, had their EMF reader in his hand.

"Go for it, Dani. Tonight was amazing! I think this was one of our best nights yet!"

Shaun, moving past Jesse with his hands full, laughed.

"And that look on Dani's face when we left her in that room in the dark? Oh man, when the tapping started..."

Jesse gave a chuckle, grabbing the last of the equipment bags and following Shaun out as they were greeted by the building's manager to lock up.

"It was great!"

Dani rolled her eyes but couldn't help herself from laughing with the boys. She wasn't the type of girl who took everything so seriously all the time. She knew how to make fun of herself and make light of situations that weren't meant to hurt her.

Jesse was the cool guy of the group, who partnered

with his best friend Shaun made a great duo in the shenanigans department. Two peas in a pod, they were often described as. Shaun was a comedian but knew when it was best to be serious. The researcher of the group, Shaun found most of the places they investigated—unless the other two had suggestions of their own.

Shaun and Jesse lived together. They had originally created a channel together on YouTube that went viral, where they played pranks on one another—often looping other friends in. Sometimes they would invite other YouTubers to join the pranks. Eventually, they found themselves progressing into checking out old abandoned properties, which at one point ended with them getting tickets for trespassing.

Later on, they met Dani through mutual friends. Dani, being an upbeat girl, described herself as sensitive to the guys and told them she'd had experiences with the paranormal. Their investigations of abandoned buildings and Dani's abilities inspired them to research and find places rumored to be haunted.

Three years after their meeting, the three of them formed a new YouTube channel called the 3 Ghost'A'Teers, where—with the support of Dani and ghost hunting equipment—they investigated properties. Usually, the team took turns researching and finding places to investigate.

But not this time.

Knocking on the door of the large house that Shaun and Jesse shared, Dani stood outside with her roller suitcase. She kept an apartment of her own across town from the boys, but this morning she'd woken from a dream that left her with more questions than answers—and the clear sense that something (or someone) was about to reach out.

She had wasted no time. Bags packed for an overnight or longer stay, something in her gut told her this was going to be more than just a visit.

The dream had left her quiet. She ate breakfast in silence, jotting the images into her dream journal—a habit she'd developed as she learned to embrace her abilities.

When Jesse answered the door, he smiled at the sight of her suitcase and stepped aside to let her in.

"Hi Dani! I'll make sure the guest room has bedding on the bed."

Smirking, Dani left her suitcase at the door. Most of the time, she gave the guys a heads-up before crashing at their place, but this time her head was still reeling with images from the night before.

"Sorry, Jesse. I know I usually call first... but I had a dream."

Jesse's eyes lit up. He'd come to enjoy Dani's dreams. Most of the time, they were a jumbled mess, but every now and then, they lined up eerily well with the investigations.

Before disappearing down the hall toward the guest room, he smiled back at her. "I'll also let Shaun know you're here!"

Dani stood near the black iron-and-wood console table in the foyer. A mirror hung above it, clean and glinting with the soft light pouring in from the windows. Dropping her keys into a decorative bowl, she caught sight of her reflection—and froze.

Images flooded her mind. She focused on a single point in the mirror, narrowing in on the sudden onslaught of dream-vision.

The sky was dark, flashes of lightning stretching like fingers across the horizon. The bolts outlined the silhouette of a towering Victorian house. With the crash of thunder, Dani flinched—jerking back at the sudden touch of Shaun's hand on her shoulder.

His reflection met hers in the mirror, a smile softened by concern in his eyes.

"Hey, Dani! No warning?"

Blinking several times, she looked away from the mirror she'd accidentally started scrying in. Reaching up to pat Shaun's hand, she laughed.

"Well, you know me. Sometimes I like to surprise you guys... I have something to tell you later. It's content-related."

Glancing back at the mirror, Dani felt her mind drift again—back to the flashes from her dream, the vision that clung to her.

Overhearing the conversation, Jesse returned from the hall. "Oh, that sounds amazing. I can't wait to hear what the universe brought you. Our views have dropped a bit—we need some fresh content."

He passed Dani, hoisting her suitcase effortlessly onto his shoulder.

"Shaun and I were talking about doing a week-long road trip—hit a bunch of haunted spots and make a series to release for Halloween. Give it a cool name."

As Jesse disappeared into the back bedroom, Dani followed Shaun into the kitchen. It was sleek, black and chrome. She plucked an apple from the marble bowl on the counter.

"I think that's a great idea. Honestly, I could use a week or two away from this city."

Shaun took a barstool at the counter, striking a relaxed pose. "Great! We've been reaching out to the locations we scoped out the last few months. A lot of them said yes. Just waiting to fill the final spot."

Jesse rejoined them, grabbing an apple too. He took a bite and grinned, mouth half full.

"Well, maybe this dream you had will lead us to the final scary place?"

Dani looked down at the apple in her hands, then leaned against the counter and took a deep breath. Her gut ached. She had known the answer the moment she woke up—but she desperately wanted to doubt it.

The later the night got, the weather changed. Lightning flashed through the curtains of the windows as the trio continued their investigation.

Dani still had the massive pit in her stomach as they joked around and did their work, catching some seriously wild activity. But now they were moving into one of the hottest spots in the entire estate: the massive dining room—said to have hosted family feasts and, more importantly, the sabbats where they did most of their casting.

Large raindrops began pelting the house as the wind picked up. Thunder crashed now and again.

The first clash of thunder sent Dani jumping and shouting, giving the guys a solid laugh. All of it, of course, was caught on camera.

"Oh man, Dani! That was amazing. That is definitely

being cut in," Jesse laughed as they stepped into the large dining room, his flashlight sweeping over the old furniture.

"I can't believe they were able to track down some of the heirlooms for this place. Can you imagine restoring it?" Shaun found a place on the floor and sat with his EMF reader, setting it up in the center near the dining table.

Jesse checked his watch and sat nearby, while Dani set up her cards, placing them upside down in a circle around her.

"Now that we're in the dining room—said to have hosted many of the witches' sabbats—Dani is going to do a reading with the ghosts. Or try to," Jesse said, finishing his piece for the camera before panning toward Dani.

She sat cross-legged, her head bowed. Shaun began asking questions, and Dani hovered her hands over the cards, feeling for the right ones to flip.

"Are you angry that we're here in your home?"

Dani's hand moved freely over the blacked-out cards, then quickly flipped one. It read: *No.*

She looked over at the guys, waiting for another question. One by one, she continued turning cards. Each question gave her goosebumps up and down her arms.

Later that day, Dani found herself sitting across from the guys in the recording studio built into the basement of their house. This was the space they housed most of the equipment they used for their investigations and their editing for their social media channels.

Sitting on the edge of the chair that sat across from a matching couch, Dani's hands combed through her long dark hair as she sucked in a deep breath, calming herself. Shaun and Jesse sat waiting in silence, but the excitement from them was palpable in the air; it made it even harder for Dani to share the almost nightmare she had the night before.

Contemplation went into whether or not she shared every little detail of the dream with them, or just the mere fact they would be filling the last spot on their itinerary. Finally pulling her head out of her hands, Dani looked up first at Shaun then at Jesse. A soft smile decorated her face, although forced.

"Okay!"

With the break in silence by Dani, Shaun felt the tension leave his shoulders and slumped back into the couch, and Jesse slapped the couch.

"Dani! I can't handle the suspense! Out with the dream already!"

The lightheartedness of the guys always had a way of making Dani feel the same, giving her a positive grounding on the earth around her when she felt her abilities pulling her away.

"Okay, okay!"

Laughing a moment, Dani had built up enough courage and decided to only share the important details needed at this moment. Reaching over before Dani could start her speech, Jesse reached for a small remote that would turn on the camera that was expertly placed in a spot that could see the staged seating area. Giving the slightest of cues to Dani, she kept her smile.

"So as you guys know, I had a dream last night that wasn't like other dreams. This one was foretelling."

Giving a dramatic pause, she looked at the camera and back to Shaun and Jesse.

"In that dream, we received a phone call from the caretaker of this very old Victorian-era house, where I am not really sure."

Pushing a loose piece of her hair behind her left ear, she shifted her gaze between the guys and the camera.

"Not many details of the location of this house came to me in the dream, but I think I might know what it looks like if I saw a picture."

Sitting up in a practiced dramatic pose for the camera, knowing that this would be edited along with other bits and pieces that get recorded into their show, Dani continued to share about her dream with the camera.

After that day, Dani had shared what she felt was necessary of her dream with Shaun and Jesse. The three of them had planned out their week to two-week-long adventure across the states investigating haunted properties.

The three of them deemed their series "Tales of the Dark," a week dedicated to some of the most haunted places across the United States. The first episode announcing their trip of horrors followed a local haunt. They had planned to release each investigation leading up to Halloween.

The final location promised by Dani's dream hadn't been brought to fruition yet, but they held onto the belief that somehow it would pull through as they planned their stays.

Many people wondered what brought them the fame among all the other groups that did essentially what they were doing full time. Teenagers related to them, and they had a way of keeping it on a level for them. Who else would sponsor gear for teens and spark them to buy useless stuff?

Shaun finished loading up the SUV they had been using to travel from location to location. Their second stay had gone without a hitch. Everything they wanted was happening without any issues.

The group had continued to keep in close contact with the other locations, making sure that nothing changed, and Dani continued to have dreams—each one having something to relate to the location they were in line to investigate.

Journaling every morning before meeting up with the guys, she would find herself reflecting on the dream foretelling of the jackpot of all locations. Dani could tell there was excitement, yet a tinge of anxiety, building up in both Shaun and Jesse about the last investigation. She could hear them talking among one another about a possible backup in case what she had told them didn't happen.

While Shaun had loaded the vehicle, Dani sat on a support wall watching, her fingers carefully picking at one another, her eyes glancing down every now and again. Jesse returned to the SUV with the last of their equipment. Helping load it, Dani moved to get in the back seat.

Sitting in the backseat behind the driver, she turned to look over the seat at Shaun. "Look, I know you guys are talking about an alternative if my dream doesn't come true." Holding her hand up to stop Shaun and Jesse, who now stood in the hatch, from talking, she continued, "I know the call is coming. I can feel it. I am trying really hard not to second guess myself, but I can hear you guys talking."

Feeling a wetness threatening to build up in her eyes, she blinked three times before continuing. "If that call doesn't come tonight when we hit the hotel for our next destination, then we go to the alternative place and I will make the calls myself." Turning away from the guys, she sucked in a deep breath, letting it out slowly through her lips. It wasn't often she let her emotions out of check with the guys, but she felt like she was letting down the Three Ghost'A'Teers.

Jesse left the hatch to get in the driver's seat, and Shaun closed the hatch. Once they were both in, they turned to speak. Jesse turned slightly, using the rearview mirror to see Dani.

"Look, we haven't lost faith in you, we just want to have a plan in case."

Shaun nodded, his baby blues smiling at her.

"Yes Dani, it is all that it is. We believe in you, and not once have you let us down."

With that, they all took off for the road leading to their third destination with hopes that, for sure, her dream would come true.

Two days later, the trio made it through their third haunt and to the hotel for the fourth destination. Sitting in the lounge area of their conjoined rooms, they quietly worked on editing pieces of their investigations, preparing to release the first of their "Tales of the Dark" with their fans.

Exhaustion tugged at the edge of their eyes as they carefully made the perfect edits, cutting in the clips of their recordings. Making the process go faster, Shaun and Jesse sat next to one another on dual laptops, working together.

Dani sat opposite from the guys, sipping on an iced coffee with her fingernails tapping lightly on the back of her phone case. A weird feeling took her by surprise, making her feel almost nauseated, as if something in the back of her mind told her to say something to Shaun.

"Shaun?" Her eyes looked up from the iced coffee in her left hand. She had stopped in the moment of nausea, focusing, wondering if it was paranormal or illness.

"Where is your phone? I think you need to have your phone near you."

Shaun looked up from the laptop burning his legs, the sound of the fans going in the machine as he used the downloaded programs to upload the finished products.

"I think my phone is on the kitchen counter..."

Dani watched as his eyes shifted to the little hotel kitchenette behind her. She stood up quickly with coffee in hand to retrieve her friend's phone.

The moment Dani stood, the phone in question started to ring—Shaun's chosen ringtone, "Final Fantasy 7 Theme Song." Shaun and Jesse froze in the moment, staring in the direction Dani was heading. She now sprinted over hotel furniture to snatch the phone in hand.

Staring at the screen a moment, Dani was met with Shaun at her side, taking the phone from her hands. Shaun touched the screen of the phone, answering the call. With the phone to his ear, he turned to watch his friends as he spoke.

"Hello?"

With the first word spoken, Shaun's posture changed as he moved to find paper and pen. His voice also took on a more professional tone as he confirmed he was part of the paranormal investigation team "Three Ghost'A'Teers."

Jesse had set his computer on the coffee table to come stand next to Dani, his eyes meeting hers.

"How did you know?"

It was quite bizarre for her to be this accurate. Usually, the only information she shared was so vague from her dreams. Jesse, in that moment, didn't want to admit that he was a bit freaked out by his friend's gift, but also he felt the rise of adrenaline and excitement.

Shaun finished the call as he wrote down the address of the establishment they were being invited to investigate, and other details given by the owners. Ending the call, Shaun stood over the piece of paper, dropping the pen. He turned to look at Jesse and Dani.

"You won't believe this."

Shaun sounded almost breathless when he spoke to the two of them. The moment of the call almost felt unreal to him. A brief moment of silence struck him as he searched for the right words to share the news with them. Jesse felt anxious for the news; Dani felt a gut ache growing deep inside her.

Jesse couldn't wait any longer as Shaun searched. He rushed up to his friend and gave him a playful punch in the arm.

"Enough with the suspense, dude!"

Shaun laughed as he snapped out of it, rubbing his arm.

"Alright, alright!"

Walking around to grab one of the cameras, he set it up on the tripod and cleared a place for them to record.

"First! We record this news so we can use it in the reveal. This is just too good."

The three of them smashed themselves into the couch with the camera ready to record. Shaun shared with their audience the amazing news. With the camera on Shaun, in the middle of Jesse and Dani, he leaned forward.

"Hello Teers! We have some amazing news! First, Dani, explain what happened."

Leaning in a bit as Shaun leaned back, Dani went to describe the feeling she got about the phone and how she somehow knew Shaun's phone was about to ring. With the story shared between the three of them to their audience, they continued to share the great news.

"Now!" Shaun spoke. "I would like to share with you the haunted property that has *never* been investigated—until now!"

The other two sat in suspense with the audience, smiling for the camera.

"We are investigating the Red Willow Estate in Colorado! They say that back in the Salem Witch Trial days, a family escaped persecution traveling to Colorado, built an estate, and survived. Some say that the long line of witches still live in this area, that the house is protected. Some pieces of their practice had been found and made part of a museum."

Jesse leaned in. He had done some quick searches on the house with what little information he could find on the museum itself.

"What was shared is that many of the guests experience touching, whispering, and other paranormal experiences. We are excited to be the first to share this with you!"

Wrapping up the filming, the three of them sat on the couch in silence. Dani still felt the pit in her stomach. Something told her that this wasn't going to be like any of the other places they had visited before.

Standing from her place on the couch, she yawned. "Guys, I am going to nap before tonight's investigation."

Disappearing to her room, Dani found herself on her bed, staring at a deck of tarot cards. Shuffling through her deck of cards, closing her eyes as she did so, Dani found herself calling out to the universe for guidance.

As she shuffled, card after card flew out until she had a layout of six cards. One by one, she carefully turned them over. Her eyes grew wider and wider. A warning was given to her—but will she take it seriously?

Swiping her hands through the six cards she flipped, she put them away with the other tarot cards and prepared for the night's work ahead of her.

The fourth haunting produced a lot of evidence and a lot of tomfoolery by the team, as usual. As per their image for their audience, they didn't keep it totally serious the whole time they investigated a property. But they also made sure to share the accurate information based on the history of the property itself.

Some people commented on their channel in negative ways, on how the way they disregard the spirits and disrespect the art in ways will cost them, but the team always ignored or laughed off the negative feedback their channel brought.

In between the travel time and the rest time taken

between, they continued to edit and prepare their releases—
and Dani dealt with a growing illness in her gut.

Red Willow sat far up on a hill surrounded by a grove of aspen and pine trees. A few apple trees dropped their apples near the entrance of the estate. The estate itself appeared to be well kept, the long drive surrounded by an old brick and iron fence giving off a very mid-century look.

There were no neighbors for miles, as the estate itself owned much of the land and still managed it, as they grew crops that were managed freely by a soup kitchen and given to the needy.

The drive up to the house itself was enchanting for the guys in the car. To Dani, it was somehow growing the pit in her stomach into a massive watermelon.

"*Whoa!*" Shaun exclaimed, leaning hard into the dash of the vehicle as Jesse drove up to park near the stairs that led to the large double doors into the massive, near-300-year-old house.

Scooting over to the door closest to the house, Dani swallowed hard. Glancing up to the massive window on the second floor, she thought she saw a woman in dark clothing holding open the curtains. Before she could say anything to Shaun and Jesse, the woman in the window had disappeared.

The car was parked and the guys were out straightening themselves. Getting out of the back of the SUV, Dani stood awestruck by the house she had dreamt about.

Hearing the sound of the hatch being opened, Dani turned to watch Jesse retrieve one of the cameras, preparing to film their entrance to the property before meeting the property manager.

Pulling in a deep breath and gathering courage for the first time in a long time, Dani knew this time was going to be much different.

Taking her spot with the guys, the trio started their filming as the property manager of the Red Willow Museum came out to watch them. The three of them came up the stairs with the camera, cuing in the manager to come into view—the three taking turns talking as they announced their final investigation on their tour.

After the brief videography, the three of them unloaded the equipment from the back of the car and awaited their tour of the grounds. Getting the full story of the family that fled Salem and the stories of those who work at the museum, they prepared for lights out.

Shaun and Jesse were prepping their bag with all of the ghost hunting equipment, checking to make sure they had all the batteries for the cameras. Dani prepared a special deck of cards she personally made for this trip.

"Okay!" Jesse stated for the camera he held. Each of the trio had a camera; Dani's was a GoPro attached to her, while the guys carried their own.

"Tonight we have a very special treat! We are here at the Red Willow Museum. They say the halls of this estate are still walked by the original matriarch who had the estate built—a family who escaped the Salem Witch Trials."

The three of them did what they were best at as the Three Ghost'A'Teers and played their roles for the camera, going from room to room setting up their ghost hunting equipment and asking their questions.

The later the night got, the weather changed, and lightning could be seen flashing through the curtains of the windows as the trio did their investigation. Dani still had the massive pit in her stomach as they continued to joke around doing their work while getting crazy activity, but now they were moving into one of the hottest spots of the whole estate: the massive dining room said to hold feasts and where the family did most of their casting during their sabbats.

Large raindrops started falling against the house really hard as the wind picked up. Thunder crashed every now and again.

The first clash of thunder sent Dani shouting, giving the guys quite the laugh—all of it being caught on camera, of course.

"Oh man, Dani! That was amazing. That is definitely being cut in."

Jesse rolled with laughter as they had made their way into the large dining room, his flashlight moving over the furniture.

"I can't believe they were able to track down some of the heirlooms for this place. Can you imagine restoring it?"

Shaun found a place on the floor to sit with his EMF reader, setting it up in the center near the dining table. Checking his watch, Jesse sat near Shaun, while Dani set up her cards all upside down around her.

"Now that we're in the dining room, said to have hosted many of the Witches' sabbats, Dani is going to do a reading with the ghosts—or try to."

Jesse finished speaking into the camera and panned it

towards Dani. Sitting with her legs crisscrossed, her head hung down. Shaun started to ask questions, and Dani would hover her hands over cards, feeling out the right one to turn over.

"Are you angry that we are here in your home?"

Dani's hand moved freely over the blacked-out cards, quickly flipping it over to reveal an answer.

No.

Dani looked over to the guys, awaiting another question. One by one, she flipped cards. Each question gave her goose pimples up and down her arms—and suddenly she jerked her head back involuntarily.

"Ouch!"

Reaching back to pull her hair over her shoulder, she rubbed the back of her head where the hunk of hair was lifted and pulled hard.

"Oh my god!" shouted Shaun. "Did you catch that on camera, Jesse?!"

Feeling another stinging sensation, Dani quickly pulled all her cards together and put them in the bag between her and the guys. "I am done! Done!"

Starting to get up on her feet, the guys started to get up with her. "Wait... what happened, Dani?"

Before she could say anything more, the three of them heard something on the other side of the room go flying off a side table.

"Whoa... whoa... Did you hear that?"

Jesse stood up, turning his camera in a nearly 360-degree view of the room, catching a dark figure leaving the doorway towards the hall leading to the front foyer.

Another flash of lightning from outside lit up the room,

allowing Dani to see the whole room in an instant. Shaun was now standing with the EMF reader, watching it spike up in a few places and then drop.

Dani stood near Shaun, staring toward the doorway to the foyer. Her body felt tingling. Jesse looked at his watch. "Let's call it!"

Dani was relieved by what he said. She couldn't remember parts of her dream, but knew by how she felt from it that it didn't feel right in the end.

Shaun smiled at Dani. "I agree. We got some freaking amazing activity tonight—and it is raining. We should head back to the hotel."

Both of the guys started to take their equipment to the foyer, where the front double doors led to their vehicles. Dani followed suit.

"I'll start taking the packed stuff out while you guys finish up?"

Dani lifted her own bag and started for the door. Jesse looked back as he started to pack up his cameras. "Sounds like a plan to me. The quicker we get out of here, the quicker we can get some sleep!"

Nodding in agreement, Dani opened the right door, watching the rain pouring over the shiny black paint of their vehicle. Stepping through the threshold of the door, Dani sprinted towards the SUV. Reaching for the handle, she pulled the door open, throwing her backpack in and her whole body into the seat.

Before pulling the door closed, she looked up to the window where she saw the woman earlier that day. Sitting in the dark of the car, she heard someone take a deep breath.

She knew the car was empty.

Sitting forward suddenly, she asked, "Who's there?" Feeling her skin crawling and her heart pounding, Dani threw the door open and ran for the house.

While Dani took her bag to the car, the guys stayed busy packing up the rest of their equipment. Shaun and Jesse laughed about what they joked about on the investigation and did a few impromptu filmings as they packed up gear.

The two of them kept one camera out because, as they continued to prepare for their departure, the activity seemed to ramp up more and more.

"Shaun, I am not going to lie, but I am ready to leave this place."

Shaun did the nervous laugh he did when things were not fun anymore. "Same, dude. Did you see Dani's face when we were asking all those questions?"

Jesse turned to face Shaun, who stood a foot from the dining room doorway. "She was changing, and you could tell something was wrong when asking those questions."

Checking his phone, Shaun noticed it had been twenty minutes since they last saw Dani take her bag out to the car. Sometimes she was known to take a five- or ten-minute break to breathe before returning to a place of investigation, but she hadn't come back in.

"Jesse, I think we should go check on Dani. It has been a while since she went outside."

Jesse started for the door with Shaun, who moved away from the dining room. Pulling the door open, Dani stood in front of the door with her head hanging down.

At first glance, they saw their friend in the rain.

Stopping in his footsteps, Shaun grabbed Jesse by his sleeve, pulling him back.

"Dani?"

Jesse looked back at Shaun, then to Dani—to see another woman's face overlapping hers. The rain fell all around her but didn't touch her. Pools of black swallowed them whole as a wail left her mouth that made their souls cry.

Shaun and Jesse dropped back against the floor hard as Dani stood before them not as herself but as the lady in black, her hands moving out and up, showing that not even the rain could touch her.

How could their cameras dare capture her essence?

The Doctor

The sky had been dark with a haze of white as most winter nights had, the cold bite close to the flesh as large flurries of snow flowed softly to the ground. One by one the flakes touched down, kissing the scorched earth, covering the marks left behind by a war-torn people. The stark white of the snow against the burnt ground painted a picture of beauty forgotten, as broken pieces of war left behind slowly rotted away under a soft sheet of white.

Pacing back and forth, a few men and women wrapped in the faded colors of their army carried rifles slung over their shoulders, holding more weight than they let on. Heads hung low, only raising now and again to acknowledge one another or to look where trained; to miss another enemy could mean certain death. Deeply sunken eyes, etched faces, and dug-in trenches of stress marked the deprivation of sleep. For years upon years, war had ripped and torn through the world, driven by greed and prejudice. Whether hundred-year-long holy wars or governments protecting resources under false pretenses, humanity continued to kill one another over reasons that still bring philosophical questions to the minds of intellectuals.

Hunger and poverty followed the longer wars dragged

on. Technology gave them new ways to destroy each other. The internet allowed them to tear one another down in unseen ways and birthed the hacker, a new brand of warfare. Fingers pointed across borders for election interference, secret theft, and scams targeting the elderly. And then, one day, it ended. EMPs detonated worldwide, silencing the internet and collapsing governments from the inside out.

Sam found himself, like most nights, on watch, leaning against his post with his rifle over his shoulder. Watching the snow fall over the rotting vehicles of the world's past, the bombed craters filled slowly like bowls of ice cream dreamed about by those who remembered a world where ice cream shops still existed. Reaching out a fingerless-gloved hand to catch the falling flakes, his eyes fell to the empty field before him. Just across the mined field lay an enemy that still attempted to shoot at them from time to time, occasionally sending someone over dressed in an improvised bomb.

With technology a scarce item in this world, many warring people turned back to the old ways before the age of computers. Even now, they found it hard to process the materials needed to continue fighting. Many of the surviving humans either abandoned posts or died of hunger or disease, having killed off most of the people necessary to keep their species going. If any high-value individuals, such as doctors, were found, they were taken into "custody," which made it harder to find new people to join the army. Survivors avoided battle companies, often running when the military passed through. It had become custom to question everyone's past professions.

Pulling himself out of his thoughts, Sam pushed from

his post to move to the other part of the partially covered guard shack, where he watched the desolate ground below for enemy movement. Hour after hour passed without incident. Sam continued to pace the shack, trying to keep his mind focused on the task put before him, as he did every night: staying awake. He picked up a beaten-up clipboard that held papers with faded lines and scratch marks from shifts before him, reviewing the checklist of the few supplies issued to guards.

Sam did what he was supposed to do as a soldier of the last American Battalion. In his downtime, he collected old journals—even partially used ones—preserving the writings of those before him. He used the blank pages to record what he had seen since being forced into the army. Being in the army was not a choice in this post-apocalyptic world: either you survived in the army, or you ran and hid from the armies still fighting.

On this particular night, Sam brought with him a small, worn leather-bound journal he had found in a collapsed house on the outskirts of a town he'd patrolled a month earlier. There had been some writing in it by a young man, recounting how his therapist had recommended journaling as a way to work through his problems. Sam hadn't read much, as some pages had been washed out by rain and water damage. Still, he salvaged any paper he could; paper not owned by the army was rare.

Shifting his feet slightly, Sam leaned over the railing that kept his body from falling. Looking out over the field, he squinted at what he thought were the figures of people moving. Reaching for the beaten-up binoculars around his neck, he looked carefully but saw seemingly nothing. Sometimes, he secretly hoped to find something during his shifts. Maybe something exciting would happen.

"Don't think things like that," he muttered softly, just in case his replacement was coming up the ladder.

Peeking at his old military watch, it was five minutes until the end of his four-hour shift. Soon, he could catch two or three hours of sleep before being required to complete other duties. The creaking sound of the ladder gave way to the next guard's approach. The whining of metal under weight made Sam tense. He hated ascending and descending the tower—if it wasn't a stray bullet that would take him out, it would be the bolts failing on the ladder.

The head of a woman finally appeared through the opening in the floor of the tower. Pulling herself up, she reached for the checklist Sam had already reviewed. "Ready to be off this old post?" Her voice was deep for a woman's, her eyes hard under the worn military cap as she glanced at him. Sam removed the binoculars from his neck.

"Yes, and I'm happy to report my four hours of watch went uneventfully. I hope yours does too, and that we keep it that way."

He set the binoculars on the plywood desk, picked up his canteen, and fastened it to the back of his utility belt. Reaching inside his coat, he touched the small leather-bound book in his pocket before finishing the handoff of equipment required for guard duty.

ater that day, Sam found himself preparing alongside a small group of other soldiers for a patrol through the small town that lay three kilometers from their base, on the line they held between themselves and the enemy. Each of them pulled on worn-out Kevlar vests that had been shot a time or two—pieces of military armor recycled through the years, despite the fact that the more they were shot, the less likely they were to stop a bullet.

Part of the world they lived in, unfortunately, meant recycling clothes and other items from the fallen around them—even compromised military equipment. Pulling the straps tightly around himself to secure the vest, Sam moved over to another soldier struggling with theirs.

"Let me get those for you."

The other soldier didn't say a word but turned slightly, lifting their arms to allow Sam's hands to work. He pulled the thick straps with military-grade Velcro, securing it all in place. Looking the slightly shorter man over once, Sam tapped his left shoulder.

"Alright, good to go."

Watching the dark-skinned man reach for his rifle and sling it over his shoulder, Sam took his cue to follow the rest as they picked up their issued weapons.

The platoon Sam was a part of was made of six—two females and four males. Each of them knew the area well and were often paired up for this patrol. Sam fell into the rear behind the short, stocky female with thick black hair. They called her Lorna—and she was mean.

Lorna didn't like small talk. She kept to herself on

patrol. She was serious outside the safe zone. The last time Smith, their leader, had tried casual conversation, he'd gotten his ass chewed. Sam, on the other hand, would pass time chatting here and there, but he had a kind of paranoia about it that made him follow Lorna's lead—total watch when they left camp.

Genna was slightly taller and broader, a woman who took pride in bodybuilding. She often challenged the men. She wasn't girly and wasn't shy about preferring women.

Then there was Duke, a tall white man of self-claimed Scottish origins. He had dark brown hair, but his beard ranged from brown to deep red with hints of blond. Duke carried a ridiculously large knife in his boot and laughed in danger—said it was just how he reacted.

Kaiser was a medium-built European man, overly polite but knew his way around a gun like the back of his hand. Of all the people in camp, Sam preferred these five. They were quirky, but together, they made one hell of a team.

"Are we all secure and ready to hit the ground?" Smith shouted from the front of the group as they were preparing to leave the metal shipping container turned locker room.

Looking over the group, his dark eyes skimmed over them, stopping on Sam, who just popped up a thumbs-up. "Roger that! Let's hit the dusty trail. I'd like to make it back before dusk."

Sam watched from the back of the locker room as Smith took point, leading everyone out of the small hot container. Shuffling one by one, the five of them exited, passing Smith on the right, whose ritual was to fist bump each one of them. Lorna always gave him a dirty look before giving in to the fist bump, which usually came after some remark from Smith about giving them bad luck if she broke the chain.

The platoon paused long enough for Smith to take his place before them. Each of them shifted the straps of their rifles on their shoulders as they started for the main gate of the camp, which would dump them out onto an old highway road.

Like every other patrol day before, they would follow the road the three kilometers east to the town that, to their knowledge from the last patrol, had been abandoned. Every visit to the town, they would go into some of the same buildings to get supplies if they hadn't already been exhausted, or they would start going through building by building looking for things. Sometimes they would find evidence of squatters that had long been gone, or they had missed them, but they never went any further in finding them. They didn't have the resources to search for people. If they happened to find people in the moment of looking through a building—well, that was another situation in itself.

They kept the talking to a minimum while walking to the town, each of them sweeping back and forth, keeping their eyes out for any sort of sign the enemy may have come to this side of the line, maybe buried explosives. Most of the time, the idea of improvised explosives was really a thought from the past—a past that should be long forgotten by now with the extinction of technology.

The walk never took any time at all, as it was less than two miles to the town, and this particular day it seemed to take even less time than usual. With the pace the group had taken up, they followed Smith right to the destination place for the pick of the day. Staring down at a list in his hand, he squinted at the few items he was meant to retrieve.

"Alright, maggots!" he shouted at them with a grin on his face, holding the list above his head. "We have the lists of items we are meant to retrieve. Each one of you take your buildings together as a pair and let's get this mess over with. The sooner we get this done, the sooner we're all sitting in our barracks resting or doing whatever."

Smith and Genna broke off towards the hospital. Duke and Kaiser went for the hardware store. All that was left was Lorna and Sam, whose jobs were to go into the library looking for some key books.

Meeting the gaze of Lorna a moment, Sam reached out for the list she held out to him. Looking over the list of titles, committing as many to memory, he gave it back to her.

"Alright, let's see what we can find."

Swinging their rifles over their shoulders in a ready position, the two of them walked towards the library that stood across the street from the local gas station—or at least what once appeared to be one. Scorch marks pushed out from a small crater where the pumps had blown out and fire consumed the small building.

Sam moved ahead of Lorna to the front of the building where the doors were. He knew that the doors weren't locked, as they had been through the building a time or two for past sweeps, usually looking for people who were looking for a place to sleep.

Reaching for the handles of the library, Sam noticed a difference in the settled dust on them, his eyes studying them as his hands rested a moment longer.

Lorna's voice came from over his shoulder. "What are you waiting for?"

Glancing over his shoulder at her, he just smiled. Pulling the door with a hard tug, it flew open with no resistance—odd, for someone who himself would have taken refuge in this place, he would have at least barricaded the doors.

There really couldn't be anyone here? Right?

His thoughts fell away as Lorna swept past him to take to the library shelves, her hand holding the list out into the sunlight that pushed through the massive glass windows of the building. She moved up and down the first few rows of the surviving bookshelves, looking for the books on her list, not noticing the remnants of life being in the building just moments before they entered.

A few rows back from where she had been working, three people—two women and a man—huddled together, trying their best to hide against some fallen shelves, hoping not to be seen. Sam unfortunately knew they were there before entering, but he had hesitated in saying anything to his partner. He hoped beyond anything that they were gone.

Having crossed over to the other side of the library to look for books, Sam spotted the lantern that was barely lit near where Lorna was working. Pulling his rifle up and turning the safety off, he pointed the rifle towards the fallen shelves.

"Get up!"

The sound of Sam's voice startled Lorna. She dropped what she was doing and instinctively pulled her rifle into position, moving back and out from where she stood. Feeling the sudden flush in her face, anxiety rose to the surface.

Sam stepped forward to meet the three who now

stood up with their hands held out, showing they meant no harm.

"Now! Get out here!"

Lorna's voice came over Sam's before he could say much more to the three. Her eyes scanned over the two women and the man; she noticed that one woman appeared to be carrying some devices a doctor would use.

"Are you a doctor?" She used the muzzle of her rifle to point to the woman with long red hair pulled back in a short ponytail.

The woman appeared panicked as she stood with her comrades. The man stepped forward, moving his hands. "No, no... she isn't a doctor."

Lorna stepped forward a moment with her gun pointed at the man. "I didn't ask you."

Sam could see the situation was beginning to escalate in a way he didn't want it to go. He could taste the tension in the air as Lorna shifted her rifle back to the woman.

"I asked you a question. You better answer me."

The woman shifted herself in front of the other woman, which made the man move to speak once more. The movement he made agitated Lorna. She lifted her muzzle and shot the man in the gut, watching him drop before the two women.

The smaller woman screamed out, dropping to hold the man who fought to hold all of his blood inside. The redheaded woman shed a tear before she pulled in a breath.

"Yes, I am a doctor."

Lorna turned to Sam, who now only had two people before him—the other one now fought for life. He watched the man dying before him on the floor, the smaller woman crying, and found himself meeting the eye of the redheaded woman, whose fate was now sealed with the army.

Without a word, Sam moved to pull the smaller woman off the man who was now dead on the floor. She screamed out for him as Sam pulled zip ties out of his pocket and secured her hands in front of her.

Lorna took her turn to secure the doctor and her things before they continued to look for the books that were on their list. Coming up empty-handed, the two of them moved to meet the others at their usual meeting spot in the town square.

The six of them met in the square as usual, but with two extras held against their will. Sam walked behind the two women as Lorna walked in front with a makeshift rope tied through the zip ties on their hands, pulling them.

"Well well, what do we have here?" Smith grinned as he walked to meet Lorna, who pulled their new prisoners—soon to be new doctor and friend?

"Sam and I caught these two in the library. There was a third, but he wouldn't quit interfering with this one..." Lorna nudged the redhead. "She is a doctor."

Smith's eyes widened with what Lorna had told him. "Well, let us not doddle, and get these two back to camp before it gets too late."

Smith took the lead, with Genna behind him. Lorna followed with the two prisoners. Duke and Kaiser took up their places after the prisoners, giving a good sandwich so they couldn't really find a way out of their predicament, and Sam took the rear.

The women kept silent most of the time as they walked. The smaller one wept every now and again, with an occasional yelp from a quick tug by Lorna. Sam felt guilty for pointing them out to Lorna, but if he hadn't done what he was supposed to do in there, he would have had his ass reamed—and punishment wasn't something he was wanting. Surviving in this world was hard enough as it was, but he hadn't intended on getting one of those three killed.

It seemed like the walk back to camp took longer with the two extras in their group, but once they had arrived at the camp, Smith and Lorna took the women to the commander and eventually to lock-up. Sam went to find himself some chow before turning in for some sleep.

While he walked to the chow tent, he found many of the others gave him a pat on the back for what he brought back with his group. The more praise he got, the worse he felt for taking them prisoner. Truth be told, they could have survived outside of this place if they could avoid them—the soldiers.

Sitting down at a table with a hot tray of mushy-looking food, Sam shoveled the gruel-looking food into his mouth without a second thought. Ignoring what it tasted like, he was just happy to fill the void that was his stomach.

With the daunting task of filling his stomach completed, Sam walked to the barracks where others greeted him with praise, and he gave them the fake smile in return.

"Yes, thanks!"

Sam found solace in the journals he kept. He wrote about the things that happened in his every day and about the things they sent him looking for. Now he sat before a blank page in the leather-bound book, prepared to write about the life he helped take this day, and the two who would hate him till the end of his time.

Sam made it a priority to record what had happened since he could remember it—from the time the wars started to the time he became a part of an army that refused to die with the governments that created them.

Two hours passed into the writing he had been doing, an easy thing for Sam to fall lost into—his thoughts and his writing.

Shouting could be heard coming from the common area of the campgrounds. Some people were calling for help—even shots were being fired into the air.

"What the hell?"

Dropping his pen into the journal, Sam jumped to his feet, grabbing his rifle, and followed others leaving the barracks to find what the commotion was all about.

"It's her!" Sam heard someone say as he watched others running, trying to catch a woman running through the camp.

"She got free and just ran!"

Sam pushed through the crowds of soldiers that were trying to get to where the woman had run from, to see where she was. Everyone was scrambling to find where she went. They were flipping barrels that were empty and looking under tarped equipment.

"Good to see you've come to find your doctor!" someone shouted to Sam as he moved through the soldiers to see a glimpse of red hair disappear in the direction that led towards the front lines.

He stopped in his footsteps in shock, not sure he actually saw her go in that direction—and that's when he heard it. The guard up in the tower started to ring the bell frantically, and that is when it started.

A body was seen running across the desolate, scorched earth as the sun was setting, and the enemy saw the redheaded woman as a sign to start shooting. Bullets started flying towards their camp. Explosions started to send dirt into the air—and then the sun had set.

Every one of the soldiers that had been out for the excitement of the escaped prisoner was now scrambling to take up positions of fire against the enemy. A full-on assault of a magnitude not seen in years started before Sam's eyes.

Feeling the blood fall from the skin of his face, he stood in place, feeling people bumping into him as they pushed him around, trying to get in position for fighting. Swallowing hard, Sam felt someone hit him in the face. Reaching up to touch his nose, he found blood on his two fingers.

"Wake up, SAM! Time to go to war! This is it!" Duke shouted, his majestic beard glistening in the little light of the camp as he pulled out his knife and went running headlong into the masses.

Lifting his rifle up, Sam walked toward the assault line, hearing bullets whizzing past his head and seeing other soldiers dropping around him in death.

It was then he saw her. The woman was still alive.

Sam couldn't believe what he was seeing. She stood in the middle of the battlefield as everyone fought.

"How can that be?"

Reaching over to grab the man closest to him—to find

Smith—Sam shouted at him over the shooting.

"Hey! Do you see her?"

Pointing at the woman they had just brought to camp hours before, he watched as Smith acknowledged the woman. *"Yeah! How the fuck is she still alive? It's like bullets don't touch her!"*

Before more words could be exchanged, Smith disappeared into the crowds as everyone pressed forward.

It was at that moment Sam found himself saying aloud, "I wish all of this would just end."

Blinking, Sam found himself standing in the middle of the battlefield with the redheaded woman. This woman stood completely untouched by the firefight going on around them. Sam dropped to the ground the moment he realized where he stood, hearing the sounds of the bullets passing him to reach either side.

Looking down at him with dark eyes, the woman reached down to him with white hands. "Stand."

Looking at her hand, he felt oddly trusting of her at that moment. "Okay."

Sam took her hand and she helped him stand to his feet once more. The area where they stood seemed to be bubbled by some sort of force field.

Sam couldn't believe what was happening in the moment he stood with this woman—woman?

He watched the redheaded stranger he had helped take prisoner earlier that day start to bleed away into a blinding light, her body holding the outline of wings made of fire and gold.

"You wish for all of this to end?" Her voice was higher

pitched than before, yet soothing to his ears. "I can bring all of this to an end. I can bring humanity to the end they deserve."

The bag they thought was full of doctor instruments she had carried with her was no longer those instruments. Now she held a large glowing orb in her arms like a baby. Cradling this orb close to her body, the orb seemed to draw energy from the being that now stood before him.

Sam watched the very orb manifest from the blinding being before him. The heat of the orb brought a sensation of calm, love, and contentment.

"You mean I just take this?" He gestured to the orb she cradled.

"Yes, Sam. All you have to do is make the choice. Do you wish to give humanity the peace they deserve or keep living in this world of despair?"

Sam knew the answer right away, but he turned to watch people around him dying by each other's hands—and for what? What would they achieve in the end of all of this?

Taking that step closer to the being of light, Sam took the orb of light from her. "What do I do with it?"

She just smiled. "You don't have to do anything, Sam. You made the decision and that is all you had to do."

The warmth of the ball of light overtook Sam's body before a flash of light overtook everything around him, eventually evaporating the human race from the very face of the planet, bringing peace.

The selfless choice Sam made didn't give humanity a permanent end, but gave the Earth a new beginning in healing that it so much deserved.

Phantom Petals

It was a cold night in winter, the air was frigid and nothing stirred in the north woods just beyond the small village of Ferndale. The open field just beyond the line of trees, which was normally free and clear during the winter, sprang to life with blue ethereal glowing blue dahlias, their petals flowing open to the rise of the full moon just overhead. The glow of the flowers fell only to the eyes of the snow owls that moved overhead, looking for their next meal, awaiting the right messenger. That night, snow fell over the field of flowers, only touching the ground around them, leaving them virtually untouched like the Garden of Eden.

Amelia was just a girl of six years of age who lived on a farm not far off from the newly grown field of dahlias. Her father was a hard man who often turned to the bottle when he wasn't turning the crops. Mr. Delgado came from a land where it was harder to have farmland of your own, so when little Amelia came along, he often found he taught her the same lessons his father taught him—with hands instead of words. Her mother, meek and quiet, sat idly by.

Little Amelia was responsible for feeding the chickens and collecting their eggs every morning. On this particular morning, she found herself standing in front of a coop with feathers everywhere. Her eyes had gone wide at the sight of blood and flesh sticking to one of the holes in the coop. Getting in closer, she could see that it wasn't her fault, but in her papa's eyes, it would be.

Reaching out with her small fingers, she touched the tuft of feathers. She heard the soft sounds of chickens unscathed from the entry of a fox the night before. Hope filled her heart that if one of her beloved chickens had survived, then maybe more had too.

Amelia had gotten up from where she knelt, her small body against the chicken coop, running as fast as she could around to unlatch the small gate that allowed her in every day to where the chickens nested, laying their eggs. Frantically closing the gate behind herself, as her father had drilled into her little skull, she ignored the gore left by the fox and scooted into the enclosure, looking for the bird she had heard.

Many of the nests had been torn up and thrown about, but in a corner a clutch of hens huddled together, keeping each other safe. "Oh, there you are!" The surprise in her little voice made the chickens coo as she moved in to scoop up a black and white hen, her fingers dancing through the matted feathers.

Feeling through the mess of other chickens left behind, Amelia found that each and every one of the survivors seemed to come away unscathed.

"Amelia!" The booming voice of Mr. Delgado came from across the yard near the old front porch of the house. At that moment, she felt her heart drop into her stomach.

Setting the hen down carefully, she left the closed

enclosure, exiting the gate and latching it tightly behind her. Staring at her tiny hands on the latch, lingering a moment too long, she felt her breath caught in her chest.

"Yes, Papa!" Her tiny soprano voice tried to hold back the dread of her father's arrival. She had turned to meet the large man who now hovered above her.

"What the hell happened?!" It was clear to him what happened in the chicken coop, but he wanted to hear it from his six-year-old daughter. Slapping his hands on his legs to lean down, he got into her small fair face, glaring hard into her dark eyes.

"Cat got your tongue, girl?"

Amelia swallowed hard as her father wasted no time to close the space between the two of them, shouting already. She did her best not to over-blink or appear too nervous, as it made him rapid-fire question her, and then his hands started to get twitchy.

"A... a fox got to the chickens, Papa."

Silence fell between father and daughter as he stood there, glaring at her moments after her tiny voice gave him the answer he already had.

"And whose fault is that, girl?"

Mr. Delgado's voice was stern, lower than before as he closed the distance between the two of them. Now he stood up with his hands resting open at his sides.

Amelia's eyes moved between his face and his hands as she spoke carefully, ready to take whatever punishment would be dealt that day.

"The fox... I latched everything tightly last night, Papa! Look, it dug and pulled the fencing there!"

Turning, she moved to point at the entry point where the fox had quite the buffet. As Amelia pointed, she felt something slam into the back of her head, pushing her down into the mud and snow. Blinking two, three times, she just lay on the ground as her father's worn boots came into view.

"You don't think I can't see that?! *Clean out the mess and mend the fence!*" Gritting his teeth, sucking in a breath. "See that the fox doesn't get in again."

Mr. Delgado left his daughter lying in the mud. Reaching to touch the back of her head where he had slapped her, knowing better than to watch him leave, she stood and got to work right away.

After spending most of her morning cleaning the chicken coop, Amelia had finally earned her free time away from the farm, away from her father, and from the possibilities of him using her as a striking post when he lost his temper over the smallest of things.

Bundled up in her worn, passed-down winter coat and a stocking cap snuggly around her dark curls, Amelia skipped her way through the woods near her farm, kicking up snow freshly laid a few nights past. It was clear to little Amelia that not only was she the only one brave enough to adventure out into the woods in the midst of the winter, but the only other prints in the snow were that of rabbits and deer that call the woods home.

Already had she forgotten the smack her father had given her as she held tightly on an old, well-read book of fairytales. She found herself spilled out into the open field of blue dahlias. Her eyes grew wide at the sight of the beautiful flowers. She smiled ear to ear as she moved to dance among the ethereal flowers that were untouched by the snow all around them.

Clutching the leatherbound book to her chest, Amelia spun around in circles through the flowers. Each one of them moved and swayed with her, untouched by her presence. Dropping back into the field of flowers after all the spinning she had just done, Amelia rolled onto her side with her book out in front of her. The flowers around her seemed to move inward as if curious to see what story she would choose to read out of the large book of fairytales.

Flipping the worn cover of the book open, Amelia settled on the story of Snow White and the Seven Dwarves. Reading the story aloud for the flowers around her, she had a large smile over her face. Unaware of the meaning the flowers held, the little girl of six continued the story of the princess whose evil stepmother disguised herself as an evil witch with a poison apple—with the one bite that would put the young woman into a coma to never be awoken unless by the kiss of her true love.

Lost in the story of Snow White, Amelia had rolled over onto her belly, kicking her legs up into the air. She hadn't heard her mother yelling her name. The sun had begun to set early, as it did during winter, and the temperature started to drop. The flowers around the little girl danced lightly as she started to sit up.

Coming through the trees to the opening of the field, Amelia's mother knew she loved to play in the field when she had free time. This time, she found her daughter getting to her feet in the field of blue flowers. Staring at the scene before her, she felt the blood in her face drain away quite quickly.

"Amelia! Get out of those flowers!"

The way she shouted at her daughter wasn't normal. The fear in her voice brought worry to the surface for Amelia.

"Yes, Momma!"

Amelia scooped up her book and ran out of the field of flowers into the snow where her mother stood pale as the snow around her. Holding the book in her left arm and taking her mother's hand in her other one, she stared up at her mother's face that never looked away from the flowers before her. Swallowing hard, Mrs. Delgado turned, pulling Amelia with her, leading her daughter away from the eerie field of flowers that shouldn't be blooming in the middle of winter.

Mrs. Delgado had returned the next day to the field of flowers with not just her husband but with other members of the town of Ferndale. The mayor of the town stood in disbelief of what he was looking at. In all the years their quaint little town had stood, they never thought they would see the fabled blue dahlias—a tale told by their ancestors that when the blue dahlias suddenly appear, a curse has been set upon the town.

Some of the men and women seemed in a panic as they stood before the field. A few of the women rushed the flowers, ripping at them, pulling them from the earth, tears rolling down their faces.

"We've been cursed! What are we going to do?" one woman cried as she tugged the flowers from their stems from the ground. As each one she pulled, it was quickly replaced with a new budding flower in its place.

The way the flowers quickly replaced the damaged

ones just baffled the citizens as they watched the distraught few try to destroy the ethereal flowers that had grown a few nights past. Finally, the town's sheriff stepped forward, stopping the two women from continuously pulling at the flowers.

"Ladies, ladies! That is enough!"

With the women looking at their now bleeding, blistered hands, they stepped aside for their husbands to wrap their arms around them.

"We won't know what the curse is until something has happened, and I haven't heard anything reported, nor have the other officers under my command. I suggest everyone go home to your families and rest. We will report to the paper if anything changes."

Stepping into the sheriff, the mayor whispered a few things to him before they dispersed to their carriages that awaited them. The Delgados left with the rest of the crowd, returning to the homestead where little Amelia tended to the chickens for her evening chores—feeding them and making sure the coop was secure.

Walking the perimeter of the coop, Amelia inspected where her father had mended the fencing where the fox had originally got into the coop the night before. Kneeling down, she ran her fingers over the fencing where it had been cut with wire shears. Once more before leaving the chickens, she double-checked the gate to the enclosure was locked closed, and she smiled at the feathered creatures that eagerly pecked at the ground, eating up everything she had spread about for them to gobble up.

"Goodnight, chickens!"

Looking up to see her parents appearing through the trees of the woods, Amelia stood by, awaiting her mother's arms to swoop around her.

"Dear Amelia, let's go in for some supper, and then it's time for bed."

Glancing up at her father, Mr. Delgado had a hard look upon his face and didn't once look down to make eye contact with his daughter.

Once inside for dinner, Amelia went into the wash basin in her room to clean up—using the wash rag left next to it to clean her face and hands—before she returned to the dinner table. Sitting down for dinner, Amelia watched as her mother moved around and dished everyone's plates, starting with her father's and then Amelia's, to end with her own.

Mealtime was particularly quiet that evening. Her parents shared very few looks between the two of them, and she didn't dare ask what was happening. For six years of age, Amelia was a very smart young girl who very much enjoyed her studies when she went to school, and she learned quickly to read the body language between her parents when things weren't right in the world.

She remembered the time the neighboring farm's bull had gotten loose and caused quite the mess in town, and her Papa had to go help them wrangle the beast. At the time of the incident, there were some whispers that someone had gotten badly injured by the enraged beast, and many people called for the beast to be put to death even though he was part of the livelihood of her neighbors. Mr. Delgado helped the neighbors fight for the life of the animal, as it wasn't its fault it was agitated the way it was. A bunch of teenagers that were looking for a thrill messed with the beast and paid dearly for their mistake. He had that same look on his face then, but somehow now it would be much different from that experience—and little Amelia just didn't know it yet.

That evening the Delgados ate their dinner in silence, with only brief moments of the silence broken when her mama asked if anyone wanted seconds, or when offering Mr. Delgado some coffee with his evening paper. Clearing the table with her mama, Amelia heard the whispers that her mother made in passing to her father only when she wasn't in the room.

The curiosity of what those blue dahlias had brought to her family and the small town grew a ball in her gut.

That night, lying in bed, Amelia stared at the ceiling, trying to devise a plan that would allow her to listen in on the conversation that she could somewhat hear muffled through the floorboards of her room.

Knowing well enough that her door creaked at a certain point of which it was pulled open, and which floorboards of the long upper hall screeched as you stepped on them, she for sure felt she could sit atop the stairs and listen to her parents who heatedly discussed the eerily bloomed flowers in the field not far from their homestead.

Sneaking out of her room, Amelia dodged all of the floorboards that made the slightest noise, hopping from quiet spot to quiet spot, finding a spot three steps down on the stairwell, clinging to the railings. Pressing her forehead into the bars of carefully carved wood, Amelia could hear her parents taking turns talking about the flowers and what they meant.

"Gerald, those flowers are a curse upon our town!" The voice of her mother was high and worried, and she could be heard pacing back and forth through the smoking room.

"Yes, I am aware of that, Gladys. We won't know what it is until something happens." Her father's voice was deep but held a calm tone to it, giving it to her father to be the calm factor with her mother.

"I am scared! Amelia was lying in those blue flowers when I found her in the field. Whatever happens, I am afraid she might be roped into it somehow."

Hearing the sudden flopping sound of her mother taking a seat in her chair near the fireplace, Amelia heard her father nearing the door.

Getting up from her spot on the stairs, Amelia ran to her room, missing one of the spots that squeaked when her weight met the board. Mr. Delgado hung his head outside of the smoking room, looking up at the now empty stairs, wondering if his ears were deceiving him as he thought he heard someone on the landing just above.

During the night while Amelia sat on the stairs listening to her parents talk over the mysterious blue flowers that had found themselves in the field near their house, the first child had disappeared in the town of Ferndale.

A little boy of just four years of age had been read the story of "The Three Billy Goats Gruff" shortly before being shuffled off to bed by his parents. His nanny tucked him in tightly under all of his covers and put out all of the gas lights, closing all the doors behind her. It was when the doors were closed behind the nanny that the boy met the face of his assailant. He found the door to his closet being opened by a troll who quickly scooped him up to disappear into the closet that led to the bridge where he lived and collected his tolls. Not a peep came from the boy as he was swept from his room, just a mess of blankets that gave away the wrestling that ensued with the appearance of the grotesque troll.

The next morning, when the nanny went to wake the boy and dress him for his breakfast with his parents to prepare him for his day of school, he was nowhere to be found. The nanny frantically searched the house up and down for the boy, hoping it was just another day of his antics, looking for him in all of his usual hiding spots, but she never found him.

The boy's parents had reported him missing to the local police, and an investigation would start for the boy, as they would have his likeness printed in the local paper. At first it just started with one boy, but days later another child went missing shortly after reading one of their beloved fairy tales. The parents were so distraught by the fact their daughter had gone missing that they started out with the accusation of their nanny, which in the end didn't lead to any arrests as there was no damning evidence against her.

Another night had passed and two more children went missing, and it could be seen how many children were starting to actually disappear with attendance in classes falling. Amelia attended her classes to find that some of her classmates were also missing, and when the children worked quietly on their assignments, the teachers were often standing in their doorways whispering to one another about the disappearing children.

It made things start to feel uneasy about the town as the citizens went about their days. Paranoia started to grow within the population as more and more children disappeared from all over. A town hall meeting was called, and every parent came to the meeting, even the ones who had their children snatched away.

The local theater was used to hold the meeting to accommodate all of the citizens that arrived distraught and ready to holler their concerns to the mayor and the captain of the police force. Some of the citizens sat in the red felt-covered chairs, others stood up fidgeting in their spot awaiting the mayor to address them. One by one, members of importance took their seats upon the stage as the mayor came to stand at a dark wood podium.

Clearing his throat to get the attention of the citizens, the room suddenly fell silent with the exception of a few sounds of women sobbing in their handkerchiefs. Standing before the room, the mayor looked out to all of the worried faces, many of them expectant of answers.

"Good evening. I am not sure how else to start this meeting off other than we are all worried and concerned as you are about the children that are going missing." He paused. "It is apparent that the blue dahlias that were found just a few miles out front of the Delgados' farm are responsible for the disappearance of the children. With that, I will give it over to Sheriff Smith."

Moving away from the podium, the mayor moved to take his seat just a short distance from where he had just stood, allowing the sheriff to take his place. His hard face looked out over the crowd of distraught parents.

Looking down to the hardwood of the podium, the sheriff stepped away and forward, open to the crowd. "We haven't figured out exactly how the children are disappearing yet, but with ongoing investigations and searching of the town and outer woods, we have yet to find the culprits responsible."

He watched the reactions of those just sitting below him, knowing it was a blow to them he hated to give, but it just wasn't something he could help. He had to reassure them that they were doing everything in their power to search for the missing children as well as those who had taken them.

"I assure you all that we are pulling all our manpower together for this situation. The mayor himself has called in reinforcements from neighboring towns to help in the search as our children go missing."

With that, the mayor stood once more, taking the podium. "Now, I won't be opening the floor for questions, as we are doing the best we can to find answers. But we will keep everyone up to date with the paper and with meetings as necessary."

Taking a glance to the sheriff, who now took a step back from the stage edge, the mayor turned to dismiss the meeting. "That is all. This meeting is at its end."

Turning to take his leave of the stage, the voices of the citizens rose as well as the sobbing of some of the women who had children taken from them. Men and women shuffled out of the theater to take their leave for their homes. Some hailed carriages and others crossed the dirt-covered streets to make their way home.

The Delgados stood just outside the theater, arm in arm. Mrs. Delgado's face was pale as she was overcome with the thought of her little Amelia going missing like the other children.

"How are we going to protect Amelia? They don't even know how they're going missing or who is responsible."

Mr. Delgado just patted his wife's hand that rested lightly on his bicep and started to lead her to the carriage that awaited them to board.

"Now, now. I will worry about that, my dear."

He didn't make any eye contact with his wife as he helped her step up into the carriage. Briefly, he looked about before getting in and tapping the top of the carriage, alerting the coachman.

After that night with the meeting, another child had gone missing after reading the story of "Little Red Riding Hood." It had been during the time of the meeting the child had been in her room reading the story when the sound of a wolf's howl could be heard just outside her bedroom window. A sudden knock had come from the window and the little girl opened it to find nothing there. The door to her room opened to a wolf disguised as her grandmother taking her away with promises of a late-night sweet.

The nanny caring for the girl didn't hear a sound but for the wolf howl just outside the house. When she had gone to look outside the kitchen door with other staff, nothing was there. Afterwards, she continued her duties and returned to the little girl to find her room empty but for a book of fairy tales lying open on her bed.

One after another, children disappeared, leaving behind traces of their captors unseen by their parents, forgotten stories lost by adults who'd forgotten what it was like to fantasize about the fairytales they once read as children themselves. After every disappearance, a piece of the story started to get left behind—a piece of clothing, claw marks, fur; even the strangest of things that would only be remembered by children who'd read the story over and over again.

The policemen were completely stumped by what they were finding, but one thing was starting to become consistent, and it was finding open or left-behind fairytale books in place of where the children had been left unsupervised. Some of the parents had even gone to lengths of setting up shifts, staying with their children at all times of the day, but it only took a moment of them reading a story to seal their fate. Whether it was right away or not, the children eventually disappeared.

Eventually, school was shut down in the town and other lessons that the children would normally participate in ended, as most of the students had disappeared. The police had come up empty-handed in every search for the children. They combed over the woods from the flowers outwards, checking every homestead they came into contact with. Everyone who didn't have children or who'd lost a child prior to the curse taking the town by surprise had been investigated with no avail. Sleep deprivation had overtaken the town, agitation was high, and everyone was at their wits' end with the events that were happening.

The mayor had death threats over everything after even losing his own child to the curse. His wife, distraught by the event, had walked into the woods never to be found again. The news of what was happening to Ferndale started to spread from town to town. Big newspapers were starting to run stories about the cursed blue dahlias and the missing children.

The month of December had passed quickly, and Christmas for the town of Ferndale hadn't happened for any of the families. It was reportedly canceled with so many of the children having gone missing.

The Delgados still had their precious Amelia for Christmas. On the eve of Christmas, they had given her a present to open. This present was special, as they had saved up for this particular gift for her. Knowing her love to read, they had purchased her a brand-new copy of fairy tales. The original book she had been reading was something that had been a hand-me-down from other families. Many of the pages were either missing or torn, leaving a few of the stories intact.

The excitement on their dear daughter's face as she tore open the gold paper wrapped around the leather-bound book brought a sort of warmth to their hearts, a sort of hope that if they'd been this lucky so far, that maybe the good Lord was looking out for them and protected their daughter from whatever it was that cursed the town. What the Delgados didn't realize was they had bought a loaded weapon for their daughter—the endgame, so to speak.

Amelia had taken the new book given to her by her

parents and fanned her fingers through the newly printed pages, her eyes trying to take in all of the images that were so carefully sketched in each story as they flew by. Looking at the time, Mr. Delgado gave his daughter a smile.

"Now, Amelia, it is time to prepare for bed. You have time to read one story. Tomorrow we open the rest of our gifts and see what Santa has brought."

Nodding her head quickly, Amelia had gotten up from her spot on the rug before the pine tree wrapped in tinsel and painted colored ornaments, running to her room clutching the book of fairy tales.

Amelia wasted no time at all dressing for bed. She had found herself snuggled up into her bed with the new book of fairytales lying on her lap. Staring down at the gold-etched letters, Amelia ran her little fingers over them one by one as if committing each gold letter to memory, her smile stretching ear to ear. Opening the book to the front page, she ran her index finger down the table of contents, outlining every story kept in the leather-bound book, stopping on the story "Sleeping Beauty."

Amelia found the page the story rested on, awaiting her eyes to read the first words in. The story was captivating, about the princess that fell asleep at the prick of a finger and slept for many, many years until the kiss of her true love awoke her. Closing her book at the end of the tale, Amelia tucked the book under her pillow before hearing her mother come in to tuck her in and turn down the lights.

"Now, my darling, time to get some rest. We have an early start to the day and then we get to enjoy a day of holiday cheer."

Tucking the blankets tightly around her daughter, Mrs. Delgado gave Amelia a soft kiss upon her brow before leaving the room.

What the Delgados didn't know was that in the middle of the night, their daughter would be lured out of her room through the window by a soft glowing green light and the soft giggle of a fairy. The fairy led Amelia out into the middle of the woods towards the field of dahlia flowers that still continued to bloom night after night, except now in the middle of the flowers stood an old spinning wheel.

The wood of the spinning wheel glistened in the lighting of the moon, calling out to Amelia, her eyes fixated on the spindle that stood sharp despite how worn the spinning wheel appeared. It was just as it was in the story she had read earlier that night before bed. It was so captivating, and yet she couldn't help herself but walk right up to it with the guidance of the fairy.

Touching the tip of her finger to the spindle, Amelia jerked her hand back immediately after the prick to her flesh. Looking at the ball of blood welling up on the tip of her pointer finger, she moved to put it in her mouth, but then she felt her eyes start to close in on her suddenly. Darkness grabbed hold of little Amelia, pulling her under as she fell into a deep slumber much like Sleeping Beauty. The fairy grew into a larger size, cackling such a laugh that would make the hair on your neck stand up.

The blue dahlias leaned over the beautiful dark-haired girl who shared their first fairy tale with them, peering into her sleeping face then up to the fairy as it swept down to take the girl into its arms. With that, the fairy disappeared with the girl, leaving no trace of her behind—or the spindle, for that matter.

With the last story told by the child who started it all, the blue dahlias turned their faces to the sky just under the light of the moon, taking in their last view of the night sky. Blue petals began to fall from the flowers that brought an eerie sense of beauty yet pain to the town of Ferndale. Each one floated away, glowing with what remained of their eerie blue glow.

Reemergence

Shear panic overtook her as they ran together, occasionally losing track of one another's hands. They ran with groups of other people who too were trying to escape the devastation brought on by the war. The fear radiated in the air around them was nearly palpable. Her heart raced as she held her free hand against the right pocket of her coat, protecting the most important piece of life she could think to bring with her while trying to leave behind everything she knew as a human being.

The couple was out in the open with others, trying to dodge the drones that sought them out amongst the other beings, looking to bring them into captivity forcefully. The idea of humans turning on one another wasn't an odd concept, since they had been fighting wars against each other for hundreds of years over things like race and religion. Now things had escalated.

Those of the human race that wished to free themselves from the oppression sought the help of the other races—the ones that could smuggle them to lands where humans were no longer welcomed due to their destructive tendencies. Exceptions started to be put into place for the ones that wished to be free, for the ones that wanted to live and thrive with family.

Ben and Alexandra were no different. They had tried for years to have a family, but the government under the human race was too controlling and kept medical help from Alexandra that would help her conceive a child with her husband. They had been met time and time again on the streets with abused power by government officials, and witnessed innocents die at their hands. Now they took a great risk of leaving their homeland, trusting the "other" races to save them from their own kind.

Ben stood speaking with a man in a dark lit room covered by a hood. He spoke in such a low tone, allowing only the two of them to hear what he had to say. They huddled close to the man as they leaned in, allowing Ben to pass over a dark yellow envelope that had obviously been shoved in and out of his pocket one time too many.

"The Vampire Tavern. That is the key to getting out of here. They're the ones helping smuggle humans out of this town. You must meet with the bartender at midnight, at the opening of the establishment in the mass transit station, and state, 'Where can one give a donation?' They will take care of the rest."

Looking around, Alexandra kept an eye out for anyone who would enter the back room of the bar where they were currently meeting the man who held the key to helping them get out of their home country. The very thought of leaving their homeland put a pit in her stomach, but the way they had to leave wasn't how it used to be.

Their government put a stop to all international travel,

only allowing travel for government officials and for trade situations. Too many civilians who had tried to flee the country in the beginning had been shot dead at the borders. Now it came down to other species smuggling them out carefully, although sometimes it didn't go as planned.

Worry always sat in the back of Alexandria's mind. It was like a plague on her mentally, and she found that she sat in her thoughts, overthinking every little detail of their plan as they were working to put it into play. Looking into mirrors, she would swear that with the way the lighting hit her head, she would see strands of silver-gray hairs sprouting on her scalp.

Finding herself once more inside her own thoughts, she turned to find the transaction finally complete and Ben reaching for her left arm. The grip of Ben's hands had a way of grounding her back into reality. Taking a deep breath, she leaned in to hear what he was about to whisper to her.

"In two days we move on to the mass transit building. We have to be there by midnight to catch our ride to the next station."

Nodding furiously to everything he stated to her, she felt a knot developing in her throat. Everything they were about to attempt was at such a great risk—the number one being their lives.

Checking the watch on his left wrist, Ben nodded towards the exit at the back of the bar storage room. "Time for us to leave. We've waited the instructed amount of time after the meeting." Clearing his throat softly, he looked her straight in the eye. "We should be safe to leave now."

Trust was something they held strongly between one another, and it only grew stronger the more and more they put their lives on the line to get out of their homeland. Love, trust, and utter defiance against anyone who would hold a life of total happiness out of their reach.

The next morning, Alexandria woke to Ben sitting on the couch across from the bedroom doorway on the phone. The two of them had taken large sums from their accounts for a "purchase," they told the bank, leaving just enough to pay each of their bills one last time. They had to make it seem everything was normal, that nothing drastic changed, that they simply disappeared.

The plan was to ditch their phones at a store's dumpster five blocks from their destination. Of course, they would take the SIM cards and snap them. They had been walked through the process of what to do on their final trip towards freedom, towards reaching happiness.

Stretching, Alexandria watched her husband from where she sat up in the bed. Her line of sight of him was perfect. She knew he was scared, but he did his absolute best not ever to show it around her. Sometimes, at night when he thought she was asleep, she could hear him in the other room walking through their plans. They had tried far too long to start a family, and he promised her that he was going to give her the happiness she deserved—and the child they dreamed of.

Ben set the phone down on the couch cushion next to him. Looking up and noticing his beloved, he smiled and motioned towards the kitchen with his thumb. "Coffee?"

Nodding her head furiously, she said, "Oh yes, please!"

Ben knew his wife well enough to know that the

mention of coffee would promise her escape from the warmth of their bed. All the mornings in their past, he worked at trying to convince her to leave that bed—breakfast, shopping sprees; no, it was always the promise of some bougie coffee that worked. He loved that dirty bean water was what drove her, and he didn't care how much she spent weekly on coffee, only that it made her happy.

Leaving the couch to start the coffee he promised, Ben leaned back to shout, "Breakfast?"

Alexandria had slipped from under the covers to pull on her favorite pair of jeans and a band T-shirt. "No thanks!"

Reaching up with a hair tie in her hand, she pulled up her long blonde hair into a messy bun. Turning to stare at herself in the mirror on her dressing table, she could see the dark circles that formed under her eyes from the stress of everything they were preparing for. Touching the delicate skin under each eye carefully, she reached for a bottle of special eye lotion. Looking at the label of this fancy dermatologist-approved stuff, she opened it, dabbing some under her eyes.

Finally at the couch, she was greeted by Ben with a fresh steaming cup of coffee, perfectly blonde the way she loved it. She took the goofy cat mug from his hands. Bringing the mug to her nose to take in the scent of the coffee, she closed her eyes, smiling before she lowered the mug for her first sip.

"Ah, heaven."

Turning to sit on the couch with one leg folded under her, she took a second sip of the hot liquid before relinquishing the mug to the coffee table in front of her.

"So, how did the conversation go with your mother?"

Watching Ben sit with his own mug of coffee, he sipped before answering. "It was hard to have a casual conversation with her without disclosing that I would never be speaking to her again."

Leaning forward, resting her hand on his leg, she said, "It is hard to think that we have to give up our loved ones for now, until this war is over. Until we find a way to fight back... But this way, we can give her grandchildren, and they can grow up safe..."

Squeezing his leg gently, she smiled briefly. Feeling a hotness fill her eyes, she felt absolutely terrible saying goodbye to her family without actually saying goodbye to them. Although she had already spoken with most of her family, something inside of her gut told her that her mother knew that this was the last she would speak to her.

"Alexandria, I love you, my sweet daughter. Sometimes we just need to start again and let our happiness carry us onward." Hearing those very words come from her very own mother made her very heart ache in her chest, made the pit in her stomach grow bigger and bigger.

The two of them shared a moment of silence, Alexandria picking up her coffee to enjoy the heat some more. Pulling herself back to reality, Alexandria felt a single tear fall down her cheek—a promise broken to herself: never to cry during this whole mess. Quickly wiping away the stray tear, she stood up from the couch to take her mug back to the kitchenette.

"Ben, I am scared."

She looked over the counter at her husband who sat holding his cup, staring out the far window. Watching him calmly take a sip, "I am too, Alex."

Rinsing out her mug and leaving it in the drying rack at the counter side, she returned to his side. "I know we have to do this, but there has been so much talk of an imminent attack with the resistance and the government."

Ben reached over to touch her hand. "We will be fine."

After their shared moments that morning, the couple spent the day figuring out what necessary pieces of important documentation were to be packed in the backpacks each of them were to carry on their backs. Each would pack two clean outfits and a few snacks in the side compartments. Traveling light wasn't ever in Alexandria's cards when they went on vacation, but this was a totally different situation.

Folding a black cloth over a pile of photos, tying it into place with a piece of hemp string, she put it in the front pocket of her bag. Catching Ben eyeing her from across the room, she smirked.

"They're important. I promise. Memories that can't be left behind."

Twirling the ring back around on her left ring finger, she caught herself looking down at the way the gems on the bands caught the lighting as she remembered to breathe. Catching herself in moments of thought, moments of memories they shared in their apartment. She looked around at all of the material objects they had accumulated together, and the items that each of them had brought individually to the relationship. Letting out a soft sigh, she knew it was going to be hard to walk away from everything they had worked hard to build.

Reaching to pack the last of her things next to her, she moved each item one by one into her pack. Leaving her right hand resting on the clothing just inside the bag, she stared down at it. Giving her head a brief shake, she pulled herself back.

"Welcome back!" Ben stated as he came up behind her, resting his hands on her shoulders. He knew that she had been taking on a great deal of stress with everything they had been planning, and with leaving her family behind it was going to be really hard to ask her to start a family in some place foreign to her. They just had to make it through all of the tough stuff first—fight first and relax last.

Giving her shoulders a tight squeeze, he motioned by the door where he had placed his bag to rest along with his jacket he had chosen to take on their trip.

"I hung your favorite travel jacket next to mine, and there is a place for your bag near the door as well."

Feeling his grip on her shoulders loosen, she looked over to the door as her hands moved automatically to zip up the bag.

"Got it."

Her voice was distant, but she knew he was doing his best to make it easy. Leaving her husband standing just behind the couch where she had been sitting packing her bag, she took her bag to rest near the door next to his own. Resting her head against the door, staring down at the shoes chosen and the bags, she could feel how much closer time was getting to them making the run. Anxiety—all she felt was pure anxiety.

Ben pulled Alexandria away from the door, wrapping

his arms around her waist.

"I think you should lie down for a bit. Tomorrow we rest all day and prepare for the night run."

Pulling her own hands up around her husband's, she nodded in agreement. Breaking away from him, Alexandria walked away to the bedroom. That night, the two of them slept on and off for a few hours at a time, allowing themselves the ability to rest during the day. But truth be told, neither of them had slept well in days.

Ben found himself standing at the counter in the kitchen making breakfast for the two of them as Alexandria emerged dressed in her attire she would wear that evening. She had decided that she would cat nap and do light activities like read and watch TV all day until it was time for them to leave for the mass-transit building.

"I see you wasted no time getting ready."

Smiling at him, she just walked up to him, taking the plate of food he had finished dishing in front of the pan on the stove.

"Thanks..."

Turning to walk away, she glanced back to see her husband reaching for another plate.

"You're welcome."

Ben had grown used to Alex taking things from him every now and again. This time it had a little touch of her normal playfulness, but still she was so stiff. Checking all the dials of the stove were at the off position, he moved to take a seat next to his wife to eat.

"This will be over soon..."

Watching as she clicked on the television, a banner

clicked over the top of the televised morning show that the government had received some disturbing news. Threats were being made, and in turn the other side were making their own threats. Tensions were growing higher and higher, and their own city was at great risk of a war breaking out.

Alexandria set her plate on the coffee table, letting her fork drop with a pang. "I can't eat any more."

Getting up from the couch, she went into the bathroom to run a bath. Ben cleaned up after the both of them, turning off the television and replacing it with his wife's favorite music. Going over the last bit of their gear, he prepared the bed for his wife.

"I have the bed ready for you to sleep some more."

Nodding, Alexandria laid in the bath after watching the water hit the ready line, allowing her body to sink into the steaming water.

The day passed much faster than she thought. Alexandria found herself walking down the street a half hour to midnight with her husband. Her thumbs were weaved into the straps of her backpack that were tightly around her shoulders. Her coat hung open, and she felt the weight of only one thing in her pocket.

The knot in her stomach seemed to grow the farther and farther they traveled from their apartment, and she could feel the rhythm of her heart beating as it grew faster. The heat from her body flushed her neck as they continued their trek toward the mass-transit station. The huge building was centered in the middle of the city, and it was designed to look like the old-timey train stations of the industrial age.

Moving in closer to Ben, she started to notice a few other people out in the streets—more than what she would consider normal at this hour. Dropping her relaxed composure, she reached for his arm, giving it a soft tug. Pointing inconspicuously at some of the other people coming off a side street, she whispered into his shoulder, "Does this seem wrong?"

Ben took notice of what she was talking about. Glancing behind him, he noticed a few other travelers, but then it seemed some others, who were not dressed the same, were coming out into the streets.

It was then the sirens started to blare from the big corporate buildings—the attack she had feared all day was happening.

She watched the few who had been using the civilians to blend in suddenly turn and start for a more centralized direction, reaching into black bags they carried on their backs.

Feeling her grip on Ben's arm suddenly tighten, she pulled him further away toward a park bench.

"Ben, these are resistance fighters trying to use us as decoys... we are going to be mistaken as one of them!"

It was so hard to hear her own voice as she started to nearly shout in his ear. At this point, they looked up in time to see lights shine down from helicopters overhead. The sounds of fighter jets shot across above them. Alexandria ducked when the aftershock of their engines hit them suddenly. A wave of nausea washed over her as she watched guns appear in the hands of the fighters, and they started to disappear down the opposite road.

Turning to relieve her body of what they had eaten for

dinner earlier that evening, Ben caught her by the arm, checking if she was okay.

"I am fine. Let's get out of here!"

Standing up, it was now Alexandria who took the lead, but this time she found herself running. Ben took the hint and kept up her speed. Not only did they run, but so did everyone else not trying to get caught up in the government's mess.

The sound of gunfire from streets away could now be heard, along with intermittent sounds of screaming. Occasionally, the sound of a loud explosive echoed nearby. The concussion of the explosions made the streetlights ring, and people from other roads came running—some quite filthy from crumbling structures.

The large building they were trying to reach was in view. Yards away, really.

"So close... so close!" Ben shouted, turning to look at Alexandria.

He had pulled her out of the way of a vehicle that had lost control. Ben and Alexandria fell over into the grass of a bank. Ghost white, Alexandria felt herself stand with Ben once more to see the car that nearly ran them down on its side, with people struggling to get out.

"We have to keep going, honey."

Turning to meet his gaze, Alexandria just nodded.

Running again, she felt her chest tighten with every breath she fought for. Chaos had erupted all around them— more and more fighting started to break out on the streets, and with that fighting came looters.

Finally, the couple had cleared the stairs of the mass-transit building and made it through the doors as the security officer came in a rush to lock the building down. Negotiating with a group of others trying to get to the same location as them, the guards allowed them inside. Shortly after locking the doors, they pulled down steel shutters over the glass ones.

Having stopped to watch the doors being locked, a moment of relief was felt by Ben. Alexandria, on the other hand, wasn't convinced.

Alexandria found herself in the first-floor bathroom, staring at herself in the mirror. Reaching into the running cold water, she splashed it upon her face.

"You can do this. We are almost there…"

Reaching for the spigot handles with both hands, she shut off the water. She leaned into the mirror harder, as if trying to convince herself.

Ben paced just outside the bathroom door waiting for his wife, anxious to move down to the lower floor of the building where the tavern stood, about to open for guests. They knew that it usually was an establishment that typically served a different kind, but today it was going to be the first gate toward freedom.

It didn't matter to them how odd it would look to the regulars for a couple of humans to walk through the doors. To some, it would look like a touring couple looking for a thrill.

Shaking out the last bit of her own anxiety, Alexandria left the bathroom to meet her husband just outside the door.

"Ready?" His voice was comforting. Her eyes met his own as he gave a reassuring smile.

Letting out a quivering breath, she nodded. "Yes… yeah. Let's go!"

Putting on a smile to cover her feelings of fear and

anxiety, Alexandria took her husband's hand as they moved toward the stairs. The building's elevators and escalators had been shut down due to the radical happenings just outside in the city, leaving the civilians locked down inside to use the stairs. The ones that were immobile were left to others to help them get to whatever floors they desired in the mass-transit building.

Passing a few others on the stairs going down to the lower basement level, Ben saw a crowd of people making their way toward an open tavern that was easily spotted with the way it was walled off with metal graveyard fencing to give it a different aesthetic compared to the inside of the massive building. It had large gothic pillars with electric lanterns hanging from iron hooks.

A man dressed in deep crimson suit pants and vest with a black undershirt stood at the entrance, carefully IDing its occupants. As the couple slowly made it up to the man, he looked them over carefully. Each of them handed their IDs, waiting to be allowed entry. With access granted, they casually walked up to the bar where the tender stood, thoroughly wiping out a large clear mug.

The white hair on his head was styled in one of those new-aged styles—long on the top and shaved on all sides.

"Newcomers! Welcome! Have a seat, and I will be with you in just one moment!"

The enthusiasm that rang from his voice—despite what was happening just outside the building—was astonishing to Ben and Alexandria. But what more did you expect from a being that probably lived more lifetimes than yourself?

Wasting little time, Alexandria took a seat on the stool just in front of her. Ben followed her, finding the stool next to hers to be open.

Looking around the Vampire Tavern, Ben was quite impressed with how they held to the myths humans had concocted over the centuries about their people, using it to enhance the appeal of the establishment. There were pieces of artwork created by artists about vampires on the walls, pictures of many actors in vampire roles, and props that were said to ward them off when used.

When the truth of their race came to the surface and they shared that they had actually been a huge part of the imaginative pieces about themselves to keep their kind a secret, so many scientists and historians had questions over the years. Museums popped up here and there. Artifacts and other memorabilia went into them for others to view as the vampires came into the light, so to speak.

Now other races and species came out to share the limelight with the vampires, and the world grew in ways never imagined.

With the human race always battling each other, it came down to those other races to save them from total destruction.

Ben and Alexandria had made a great decision months ago in just that—to trust their human lives to that of the vampires.

The bartender returned to the couple that were anxiously waiting at the bar for his return. He looked them over carefully, noticing the change in their body language when he returned. He knew well that the two of them were not his regular type of customers, nor were they the typical tourists—no, they were the ones waiting for the underground.

Ben leaned into the bar, making eye contact with the bartender.

"Where can we make a donation?"

Alexandria stayed still, watching the bartender for his reaction, her hands resting on her pants. The heat from her legs started to make her palms sweat. All she wanted was to finally be whisked away toward the train out of here. Were they still smuggling with the bombings and fighting going on just outside the building?

With her mind racing a hundred miles an hour, she suddenly found herself with a glass of water in front of her.

"Thought you would like some water!"

The tender had moved so fast she hadn't seen him get the water, but he did watch everyone else around them while he served them discreetly.

Alexandria helped herself to the cold water, the taste bringing her back to reality. The tavern was finally filling up with those who actually made it into the mass-transit building before the lockdown.

"Follow me this way!"

Suddenly, the white-haired bartender stood in front of the couple, motioning toward a back room where many bottles of liquor and foreign liquids were stored.

Leading the couple toward another doorway with a drape overhead, he moved a carpet that hid a hatch dropping down into a tunnel where another man awaited them with a lantern.

"Follow your guide, and he will lead you to a

new beginning."

Alexandria was the first to descend into the tunnel just below the mass-transit building, followed by Ben, who patted her backpack, notifying her he had made it.

Turning, Alexandria held a small silver case in her hand. The guide leaned in, looking at what it was she held.

"Oh, you truly are going to be making a new beginning?"

Nodding her head, Alexandria stowed away her hope of family with her husband in a place of peace. The couple followed the vampire down the tunnel, leaving behind only the soft glow of the light given off by the lantern—the light of hope.

Golden Rods and Griffins

The day was like most mid-spring days, it was warm and the sun beamed high above them. A bite of cold touched their skin with the breeze, as it caressed through her hair. Asta had met her longtime friend Gareth as they had planned a few days prior to go hunting just outside the village where they called home. From afar, she could see him standing, waiting for her. He stood staring outwards towards the woods. The two of them were determined to bring home some meat for their families due to the harvest possibly being poor. The weather hadn't been kind to the farmers, and the land around them where they planted started to dry up and crack.

Asta had a few younger siblings she was concerned with feeding. With her father in the fields and her mother tending the wounds of the other villagers, it was up to her to help.

"Gareth!" Waving her hand freely, she held a brown leather bag over her shoulder in place with her other hand. Smiling, she picked up her pace when she had seen him waiting ever so patiently for her just outside the village. "Sorry I am late! Let's get out of here!"

Briefly slapping her hand on Gareth's shoulder, she looked at his bow and the woods. "May Vion, God of Hunting, bless us with a great bounty to feed our families and friends."

Asta had dressed in leather trousers and her hunting leathers, with knee-high boots tied in place around her calves to protect against low-hanging branches. Of course, she came equipped with her own bow and quiver full of arrows, but Asta had other intentions other than to hunt.

Gareth just shook his head with a mere smirk on his face as he led his friend away into the woods, waiting to get somewhat far enough into the woods to look for deer tracks. Once inside the trees, the two of them started to look closely for tracks; but Asta let Gareth do most of the tracking. It hadn't taken long for Gareth to find the trail of a few deer. The two of them started their journey further into the woods away from the village.

A few hours had passed since the two of them started to track the deer. Asta noticed some horsetail growing along the route they had been following towards the deer Gareth had caught wind of. Kneeling down to carefully cut the stem of the horsetail with a small hooked knife, Asta started to lose track of where Gareth was as she found more horsetail to harvest. One by one, she cut the stems of the wild herb, carefully placing it into her leather bag. Turning on her heels, she noticed bloodroot growing near the base of some trees. A spark grew in her eyes at the sight of the flowers. She stood up really fast to rush over to the flowers.

Leaning down to start the harvest of the flower, Asta used the blade of her hooked knife to dig into the earth around the flower to loosen the root of the flower itself. Taking the whole flower—root and all—out of the dirt, she started to carefully place them in her bag when she felt the cold feel of steel at the side of her neck.

Feeling everything in her chest tighten at the realization of what she felt on her neck, she held her hands outward, showing the small knife held in her right hand.

A deep baritone voice came from behind her. "Don't move an inch."

A thick hand came from around her, grabbing the small hooked knife from her now loose grip. She could feel the pulse in her neck quickening with the touch of the stranger. What was happening? Was this just one man or were there more? Bandits? Or—

Horses came out of the trees around her, decorated in the colors of dark blue and goldenrod yellow. They were the imperial colors of the ruling house

Bakirtzis. The man who held the sword at her neck held the blade in place while he moved around into her view. He was dressed in silver-plated armor with the imperial crest of the griffin engraved on his chest. The movement he made was subtle but enough to allow his sword to nick her neck, allowing blood to seep from her flesh. With the location of her wound and how small it was, it certainly gave off the illusion it was much larger.

Feeling the warm stickiness of it start to run down into the top of her hunting leathers, she fought the urge to reach up to stifle the wound.

"What do we have here?" The man's voice echoed outwards once more as he now stood in her view. His scruffy beard pushed out from under the helmet he had adorned for that day's patrol, although to her and all other innocents it was viewed as a man-hunt. Although they were the guard of the imperial house sworn to protect the land, they didn't take kindly to the heathens that didn't conform to their way of life, to their gods.

It didn't take long for other guardsmen to join the man who stood with her at swordpoint. Some of them circled them, looking her up and down as if determining what she would be good for. Asta's eyes followed the men as they searched the grounds for another woman—so they hoped—or for the person whose footprints they found before they disappeared. Thankfully, it hadn't been too wet that morning, and the sun did its job drying up the earth before Gareth and she took to the woods for the hunt.

Closing her eyes for a moment, she thought about how it would kill her if she were to be responsible for her dear friend's capture or, worse, death.

"Now now..." Another man stepped up to the gruff-looking swordsman who held her at the point of his blade. "Let the little lady speak..."

Leaning forward, the red-haired man had held his helmet in the crook of his left hand while he leaned forward to examine the blood trickling down her neck.

"You've already injured her? We haven't gotten a name or where she is from?"

The *tsk* sound came from his tongue clicking at the back of his teeth as he stood straight to give that somewhat strict glare at his battle buddy.

Feeling the pressure of the blade lift from her neck, she felt the stiffness in her chest ease slightly. Looking down into her lap, Asta felt the smack of a rag hitting the thick leather of her coat.

"Wipe your neck, woman!" The voice of the man who cut her with his blade spoke after using that same rag to wipe clean any of her blood that may have tarnished his blade.

Picking up the soiled rag, she moved to delicately wipe at the cut on the side of her neck while keeping her eyes on the men around her. Glancing at the amount of blood on the rag, Asta felt not much more could be done for the cut as her blood had started to clot at this point.

Holding the rag out to the man, he just scoffed. "I don't want that back! Blood of a heathen has soiled it, best leave it to rot... No time to burn it."

What they didn't realize was that it could have been the best idea they'd left her with, but would it be in the best interest to leave clues? Leaving the rag where she sat, Asta carefully placed a stone over top of the rag to keep it from blowing away if the wind were to pick up. With no intention to keep the rag to cover the wound, she actually felt her brows raise a slight moment with a thought that crossed her mind as she was shoved from behind on all fours.

"Stand up!" The red-headed man came around from behind her, watching as she caught herself just over the stone that held the rag. Pushing herself to stand up, she met the blue of the man's eyes. "Well well, I think we are going to just take you back to the palace and let them do what they will with you."

Asta didn't have a chance to contest that decision made without her, as two other men came up beside her. One grabbed for her hands as the other moved to shove a cloth bag over her head.

A scream moved up her throat without a second thought, and it was when the first sound started to leave her lips that the back of her head met the pommel of the gruff man's sword. The blow that hit her brought a flash through her eyes before the faint feeling took over her body and everything went black.

The ride on the back of a horse as a sack of potatoes was quite rough, especially for Asta, as she couldn't see a lick of anything through the sack over her head. She could feel the rhythm of the horse's steps and eventually the way her head bounced when it took to a trot.

Finally, at some point the men seemed to have come to a stop, and the man who she rode with finally moved to check on her. Still somewhat dazed from the pommel she took to the back of the skull, Asta felt her equilibrium was off and soon she would too be off the horse.

Feeling the hands of the man around her, she quietly asked, "Where are we?"

The man paused in mid-step with her over his shoulder, not sure if he should alert the others.

"We are at a stream to water the horses, and to rest for the night."

Shifting his weight to prepare to set Asta on her feet, the man turned from the side of the horse he rode.

"I am going to stand you on your feet."

Setting Asta on her feet, the man had just enough time to pull the bag from her face before she fell to her knees in one fell swoop. The sudden crunk on the ground sent a zing of pain up her leg and back. The look that shot across her face from the fall was evident as the soldier moved to help Asta to her feet.

"Are you okay?"

Feeling the world spin a moment or two, Asta was finally able to meet the brown eyes of the man who was put in charge of her for the journey back to the kingdom of Agremenad.

"I think so." Her voice was soft in that moment, as she was afraid to speak no louder.

Asta glanced around the man to watch the other men lead their horses, some multiple, to the stream to get a drink. One of the freemen came to claim the man who steadied her horse to the water's edge. Her eyes followed the man as he came and went with the beast without a word.

"Thirsty?"

The man's words brought her back to reality, turning her mind to the canteen before realizing it was her own from the bag of herbs she had been carrying on her person. Looking down, her tied hands instantly moved to feel for the leather bag she carried.

"If you're looking for your belongings, we took them off of you before we took leave for the palace grounds. And yes, this is your canteen. We can't share our water with a heathen." His words had a bite even though his tone was semi-soft and kind.

"I see," Asta spoke as she reached with her tied hands for the leather canteen she had filled prior to leaving her home for that morning's hunt with Gareth.

The man had done her a kindness and removed

the cap for her convenience. Tipping the canteen to her lips, she allowed the semi-warm water to touch her tongue before finding its way home in her belly.

When Asta had finished with her fill of water, the man took a loose piece of rope from her wrists and led her to the stream.

"I suggest you refill that canteen. We have a day and a half ride till we get back home."

Heeding his advice, Asta wasted no time kneeling near the water's edge, refilling her canteen. Still knelt with the canteen pinched between her knees, Asta prayed to Zihses to bless the water, protecting her from any sickness.

The man now stood over her, staring, eyes widened. She glanced up, noticing he caught the tail end of her prayer. He had been kind thus far, but he couldn't stand hearing the prayers of others for their gods. Triggered by her, he leaned down, smacking her from left to right with the back of his hand.

"Don't let me or anyone else catch you praying to those gods. They're dead. And it is best you keep them that way!"

Confused by what he had said to her, Asta decided it was best to keep her mouth shut. Although she was quite devout in her beliefs, she knew that it wasn't worth her life to fight the men who were in the process of hauling her away to a land far away for gods know what.

Reaching up with the canteen in the clutches of

her tied hands, she touched the side of her mouth with the back of one tied hand gingerly. The man watched her as she came away with a little blood. The smack split her lip as the impact pushed her lip into her teeth.

Taking the canteen from her, he watched as the man who walked away with his horse returned with the beast. This time, he stashed the bottle in his saddle with one hand while the other clutched her ropes. From afar, they could hear the shrill whistle come from another one of the soldiers. The others started to mount their steeds, preparing to take off once more.

Asta stared at the man who stood before her holding her bindings, hoping he wouldn't place the bag over her face again.

"Time for us to go."

The man slid a foot in the stirrup, pulling himself up into the saddle. Holding on to the base of his saddle, he reached down with his free hand to pull her up by the ropes that tied her hands. Boosting Asta up, she swung her leg up over the rear of the mare. The soldier secured the loose rope he had pulled her along with around his waist, and with one swift movement of the reins, the large beast fell in stride with the others.

Less than an hour's time spent on horseback came to an abrupt halt when the cavalry of soldiers found that a large number of trees had fallen onto the main road—one that led to the wooden bridge built to carry them over a river too deep for horses to cross.

One of the men at the front of the cavalry dismounted his horse to inspect the fallen trees. As he started to look at the cut marks on the logs, a cry came from out of the woods—along with an axe flying into the fallen stack of trees.

The men on the horses quickly pulled up on the reins, turning them about to face the woods on both sides of the road, each of them pulling their swords from the scabbards strapped to their steeds.

"Where are they?"

Arrows started to rain down from random directions. Sparse as they were, one or two of the men took one in a body part or another.

The attackers finally emerged from the woods screaming, with old beat-up weapons—some still with the bows they used to shoot from the trees.

Asta's eyes widened at the thought of these villagers taking up weapons against the army from the imperial palace, but she could sympathize. She too was being taken from her home.

Ducking her head down into the back of the man who held her against her will, she prayed to the goddess of light. Her prayer, quietly spoken, was for them and for the villagers.

She watched as the fight quickly started—and quickly ended—with many of the rebels dead and the others in ropes.

The two men who had taken arrows were side by side. One had the arrow out of his shoulder and seemed fine. The other was in rough shape; his wound sat in the lower half of his gut.

Sliding off the horse, Asta pulled at her captor, turning her gaze to him.

"Bring my bag with the herbs!"

The man resisted her tugging and stared at her as she continued to fight to get to the wounded men.

"I can help that man!"

Turning herself fully toward the man with the loose end of her ropes, she wrapped her wrists further into the rope and gave a huge tug, yanking him toward her.

"Now!"

Finally listening, the man grabbed the bag out of his saddlebags and led her toward the man with the arrow sticking out of his gut.

Wasting no time, Asta pulled her way to the injured man's side and sat on her knees, watching the captor kneel with her bag. She made eye contact a moment before she moved to the arrow in the man's gut.

Breaking the shaft of the arrow, she pulled out some of the long strips of cloth she kept in her bag to tie the herbs together and used it to secure the arrow in place in his belly.

"Help roll him!"

Sliding the cloth under him, she then wrapped it around the remaining shaft of the arrow and tied it to the other piece of cloth. Pulling some powdered horsetail out of her bag, which she carried just in case of minor wounds, she opened the small leather pouch and sprinkled it over the man's wound.

"Now carefully help him onto a horse with another. He can be taken to a proper doctor."

Putting her herbal powder away, Asta gave the leather bag back to her captor as she stood, her bloodied hands at her side, watching as other cavalrymen moved the injured men to horses for transportation.

"What will happen with the rebels that attacked?"

Her eyes shifted over the dead, then to the roped people.

"They will meet their trials, and those who fail will go to the mines…"

With that, the man in charge of her led her away, as the rest moved the trees, preparing to lead them to the nearest temple of their gods for the night.

Late that evening, the cavalry with their prisoners arrived at a large temple carved out of white marbled stone. Outside, large figures of a female goddess stood welcoming them to the temple. Asta's eyes grew as she took in the beauty of the massive building and all the glowing braziers that burned at points about the temple.

Monks under the care of the high priestess came to greet the soldiers, helping lead their horses to the stables for a proper grooming and feed for the night, while the men in charge of the prisoners led the villagers to a large room where they could be tied up to a portion of the walls where they could be watched.

Tied up near the other prisoners, Asta found that some of them didn't appreciate what she had done. Asta felt the warmth of saliva smack her cheek as the prisoner two rows down from her spat in her direction. Glaring, they made it known that if they were alone, she wouldn't be safe.

The guides of the temple came around to all the prisoners with a small wooden bowl of stew and a chunk of bread. Each of them contemplated giving thanks, but Asta didn't hesitate. Kindness was being shown to her and the others around her despite their beliefs, and she in turn gave thanks to them.

"Thank you." Her words were only loud enough for the guide that handed her the food. The young woman gave a brief smile and nodded her head in response.

The time spent at the temple was semi-pleasant for Asta in a way, as she got to see some rites and rituals performed in the names of the Imperialists' gods, and not once did the performers of these rites call out the villagers in such a negative way like the soldiers did.

Hope sprung in her heart as she noticed so many

likenesses and similarities shared.

The trek to the palace grounds was much shorter than anticipated. The men were received by a party of stable hands and other workers ready to take the tired beasts off their hands. Other, less worn-out guardsmen took Asta and the other prisoners away to cells further into the depths of the large castle, decorated in the blue and gold of the Bakirtzis house.

Banners with griffins and the house crest decorated the corridors, alternating with plain banners. Choice pieces of decorative furniture and vases full of blooming flowers sat in deliberate places up and down those halls.

Asta sat in a dimly lit dungeon cell, chained to the wall with a few others from the group that had attacked the men. She could hear the soft moaning of others from cells down the way. Her body felt bruised and sore from the long ride to this place. What was worse was wondering what would become of her from this point on.

As the days went on and Asta was moved around from cell to cell, the guards rotated the prisoners as they were taken away to be vetted for one thing or another. It didn't take much time for Asta to find herself pulled from her cell and thrown into a room with women in white and blue garb. They quickly undressed her and took her to a large wooden tub of lukewarm water. Bathed and dressed in a brown, rough-spun dress and her hair tied in a braid, Asta was presented to a woman spectacularly dressed for a high priestess.

The woman before her was dressed in silks of white and gold. Her shoulders were gilded in plated armor shaped like griffins' heads. The eyes of the woman were incredibly blue, painted with black paint, and her markings showed where she stood in the order of their religion.

"Welcome." The voice of this woman was full of melody—she could sing even the sirens out of the sea. "Our house of gods welcomes you. Please know that you are safe here."

Asta watched as the priestess walked around her in a way that made it appear her robes moved with a mind of their own. She gestured to the statues of the goddesses and gods in each corner of the room. Words flowed from her mouth as she led Asta around the space, directing her to the story painted on the back walls and following it through a hall to another room where more of their gods rested.

The history of their beginning flowed much like the beginning of her own gods, with the exception of theirs fighting her gods for rule of the high heavens.

"See, Zihses and Eudora with all the rest of the heathen gods were failing the human race. So that is when our gods rose to power. With that, they brought peace and prosperity to our people."

The priestess and a guardsman led Asta to a very large terrace that overlooked prospering lands being worked by the peoples of the imperial country. Walking to the large stone railing, Asta leaned over to take in the whole view. It was quite astonishing to see so many people living, so many people achieving what her small village hadn't in so many years.

Taking a step back toward the priestess, who now stood three feet behind her, Asta reflected on all those sacrifices she had made to her gods day in and day out for her family—for her village.

Turning abruptly to find the priestess right behind her, Asta jumped slightly.

"See. I am your first stop in redemption, your beginning towards a life of happiness and prosperity. Only if you so choose."

The priestess held her hands out toward Asta, while the guardsman—now joined by several more—awaited the choice she would make, like many others before her.

Looking once more over the side of the terrace toward the thriving city below, then back toward the guards, Asta felt it in her—that if they could be so prosperous under these gods, why couldn't she? Why couldn't she be the first of her village? Why not someday be the way to bring them all prosperity and happiness?

The warmth of a smile grew on her face as she felt her arms lift from her sides, reaching out for the hands of the priestess. Asta took her hands, squeezing them ever so slightly.

"I will. I, Asta Sideris, pledge to honor and follow the gods of the Bakirtzis house."

A gleaming smile formed on the priestess's face as she pulled Asta in for an embrace. Letting Asta go, the priestess took a step back. "Wonderful! Now, I hear you helped some wounded men?"

Taking the lead, Asta followed the woman with only one guardsman for safety. "I did. I am a healer in my village. I was harvesting herbs when I was taken."

Glancing back at the guard behind her, the man just frowned.

"Good, good."

Leading Asta to another room, where she would join others like herself who had accepted the religion of the great imperial empire, the priestess left her sitting against the wall with the others. With so many questions plaguing her mind, Asta sat wondering what would become of her now that she had turned against her own beliefs.

It hadn't taken long till someone came for Asta and everyone else that sat awaiting what would come next now that they had accepted their new fate. The door opened, revealing a tall woman with dark black hair and skin to match. She wore gold and blue robes with silk gold cords tied around her waist.

"Hello." A simple greeting, as she stood in the door, her shadow being cast further in by the lighting behind her.

Asta sat up straight, her eyes locked on the woman who seemed elegant in the clothing she wore, and now stood with her hands folded before the people.

"I would like to welcome you all to the Imperial City. If you all would stand and follow me out in a line, each one of you shall be divided out among others like myself to take you to your new workspaces and living quarters."

Turning, the woman gestured toward the doorway before looking back to make sure everyone was getting to their feet. Standing, Asta moved with the crowd of others like herself, feeling a sudden burst of excitement yet anxious, wondering where she would be placed among her new home. Although she was an outsider, she somehow had been given such mercy by the graces of her new gods.

One by one, they all filed out of the room. Watching as groups of them were taken away by others in the blue and gold robes, Asta wondered why she hadn't been summoned yet. The dark-haired woman stood smiling, watching and waiting. Finally, she approached Asta.

"My dear, you are to follow me. I am going to take you to the healer's grounds."

Feeling a warmth grow in her cheeks, she wondered why she was the only one chosen to go. Clearing her throat, she hesitated in speaking at first.

"Excuse me. Why am I the only one going?"

Looking about as the woman started to lead the way, Asta felt slightly nervous about her new station.

"Well, it was brought to our attention that you didn't hesitate to help our injured, and that you knew what you were doing."

No other words were spoken by the woman as she led Asta away from the others. Feeling the pit in her stomach fade away from the worry, she took advantage of the small tour—from where she was being held through the main grounds to her new home.

Groups of soldiers marched together in more casual dress, each sporting the colors of the Imperial house. Archers stood on green fields, practicing their aim while shooting their arrows. The further away Asta was led, the more flora and fauna took over the grounds, and soon a large cobblestone building rose before her with a greenhouse. Closing her eyes, Asta could smell the fragrance of many flowers that bloomed at this time of year in the air.

"Am I to become a healer?"

The woman glanced over her shoulder with a smile, her dark curls bouncing as she walked. "Yes, you will learn with our doctors and herbalists. Depending on your skills, you will find placement among the people, palace, or soldiers."

This was clearly more than Asta had ever imagined, even living in her own village, living day to day trying to survive with what little they could harvest among the forest. Her thoughts fell on her family back home and everyone else that were worrying about her. Motivation to be the best filled her soul.

Suddenly they had stopped just before the massive building, and the woman gestured for Asta to go inside.

"This is where I leave you. I wish you all the best."

Bowing her head slightly, the woman turned and left Asta watching.

Turning, Asta stared at the red painted door. Reaching the knob, she disappeared inside.

A few days had passed as Asta had grown into her new role within the imperial city walls fairly quickly. She was given privileges in the garden among the slaves that were out pulling weeds and taking care of any pests that might threaten the life of the plants.

The day was a beautiful one. Asta was leaning over some horsetail, picking what she needed to dry when she heard her name yelled out. The voice was all too familiar—but it just couldn't be who she thought it was.

Looking up from the field of flowers and herbs, her eyes fixed on a man in armor. She watched as he walked toward her as quickly as he could without causing suspicion.

"Asta, it's really you!"

Emerging from the field, she walked toward the man. "Gareth?" She just couldn't believe that Gareth had made it into the imperial city without being captured. Looking him up and down, she noticed the blood on the armor.

"Yes! It's me!"

It was all so hard to believe, and then it was over as quickly as it had begun. Asta had been reunited with her best friend Gareth, a man who risked everything to rescue her—a woman who didn't need rescuing in the end.

"Gareth!"

Hugging Gareth so tightly in that clunky armor, she stopped to look at him. "But how?"

Gareth shook his head. "Not now."

He had started to pull on her hand, tugging her away from the gardens and away from the place she called her home. Looking back to the building, she started to resist the pull of his hand.

"We need to get you out of here!"

His words alone were enough to put all the brakes on for her. How could she go back now? She had put everything into the new gods here. She saw what they had done for the people. If she could prosper here, there was a possibility she could bring the new gods home to her people and bring them into a new time of prosperity, leaving behind all the poverty and pain.

Gareth turned, looking at Asta who stood resisting

his pull away from the garden, away from this place, and he saw all the pity and sadness in her eyes.

"What?" he asked.

"I can't..." Asta spoke with stillness and defiance.

It was then, for the first time, Gareth saw what she had worn—and she saw it in his eyes. She stood before him wearing the blue and gold of the Imperial city of Bakirtzis, and it was like the breath was just knocked out of him.

"No..."

It was then something changed in the atmosphere around the both of them. It wasn't just the look on Gareth's face; it was like static electricity spun between them as everything became silent.

Looking around her, Asta was frightened by the sudden frozen moment around them. The very wind ceased to exist. The sound of all the people and the hustle and bustle of workers all faded away. Not even the sound of their heartbeats could be heard.

A great being of darkness grew before the two of them, and it was Asta who appeared horrified at what she saw.

"Oh, the irony!"

The very words were not of Gareth, but of a demon that had shown himself in all his glory to Asta.

"What?"

Her voice caught in her throat as her eyes grew wide, looking up at the great horned beast who was clearly amused by everything that had just transpired.

"What is happening, Gareth?!"

She cried out as she kept her hand in his, her eyes never leaving that of the demon who laughed to itself. "I'll tell you what is happening!" The demon stood with all his twisting horns, and fiery eyes glowing. "Your pathetic little friend here offered me his soul in exchange for saving his life so he could rescue you—only to learn you do not need rescuing." The demon cackled with glee, his head rolling back with laughter.

"No!" Asta cried, tears falling from her eyes as she looked down to Gareth, now on his knees before the demon. "No... no... no!" Dropping down, wrapping her arms around Gareth, she buried her face into the back of his shoulder. "Please don't!" She wept into her arms, holding on to him.

"As heartbreaking as this is, I really should get going," said the demon, his eyes shifting with a joyful gleam to Gareth. "Time to go, boy."

Lifting her head from her arms, her sleeves clearly stained with tears, she desperately pleaded. "Take mine instead, please!"

Before she could say much more, Gareth snapped, "Asta, no!"

Her arms came off his back side, breaking the hold around his body. Dropping her gaze to him, she stared at him for what seemed to be a long moment. She just couldn't understand why he had done what he did—and even so, she was willing to give up her own soul for his.

Anger filled her eyes as she looked toward the demon once more, pleading. "Please!"

The demon laughed, wiping its clawed hands together. "It's too late!"

Looking between Gareth and Asta, the demon grinned. "It's done."

It was then Gareth had pulled her chin toward him, his eyes meeting her saddened gaze. "I am glad you're okay," his words were softened as he held her gaze. "I lo—"

Before he could finish what he was about to say, Gareth's eyes went blank. Asta watched as his soul left his body, his limbs falling limp around him.

Looking up, she found the clawed hand of the demon hovering over Gareth. His essence was being pulled out of his body.

"Who knew this ending would be so delightfully tragic! I can't thank you enough, my dear!" With those words left behind by the demon, Gareth slumped over into Asta's arms.

As quickly as it all had begun with the arrival of Gareth and the demon's interventions, time restarted around Asta and her best friend's body.

Sitting in front of the large cobblestone healers' quarters with Gareth's body laid out before her, she stood up to find that the slaves had come to find her standing over him, fists clenched. Tears had dried on her cheeks, her face red from the time spent in the moment of dire circumstances.

Looking at the slaves, she spoke softly. "I will take care of this man. He was a friend."

They left her with white canvas body wraps, and she went to work carefully pulling off the metal armor that wasn't his. Piece by piece, she set it next to his body, looking over the scars he carried from the incident that put him in the mess he paid for. Tracing her fingers over his cheeks and through his hair, tears stained her cheeks once more.

Carefully wrapping his body, tying it off with the gold cord, she stood over him, wiping away sweat and tears from her cheeks. Turning to find that the slaves had gone for the high priestess and others of the order, she found the woman standing with a procession of monks, ready to take away the body of Gareth.

"My dearest daughter, I am here to take him."

Kneeling down to lay her hand over where Gareth's forehead would be, she looked up to the woman. "Please put him in a stone coffin."

Standing, she walked to the priestess, leaning in. "He gave his soul for me."

With that, Asta left Gareth's body in the hands of the gods she wholeheartedly believed in and trusted.

Three days passed. Asta had traveled on foot to a large circle of stones that sat erect in the middle of a field surrounded by the ruins of an ancient city.

The story behind the fallen empire was one of legend. Everyone knew the story of the mad queen and her king. They had ambitions that were never satisfied, and one day they sold not just their souls, but everything that filled them, for their seats among the gods. Greed overtook them, and when they couldn't pay their debt, the empire fell into ruin, and their people died or scattered across the continents.

In the middle of the large stone pillars lay a stone slab of runes and a dial that could be turned by the hands of a mortal. The legends said that the gate to hell lay in the middle of this ancient metropolis—that opening the door would lead the desperate down a staircase to the river of tormented souls.

Asta was one of those desperate souls, and she traveled a long way to find Gareth.

Filled with sadness, anger, and regret, she bent down, taking hold of the thick, worn stone dial, pushing it with the strength of her upper body, backed by the power of her legs. Feeling the movement of the dial budging under her weight, she didn't smile. No—Asta felt a look of scorn cover her face as she prepared herself for the next task.

As the dial seemed to click into a place, a distant sound of a scream came from the thick stone of the door that resembled that of a cellar door leading down. Asta felt herself jerk backwards to the sound before she pulled the heavy door open to the side.

A rush of heat splashed her in the face. A darkness washed over her body like the first cold of winter. Shivering.

"Gareth…"

Looking deep into the opening, she waited for something or someone to greet her, but there was nothing for a long moment.

"I am coming for you."

Taking that first step into the abyss of what would be hell, Asta knew deep inside she would face that demon to take back her best friend's soul—or die trying.

As she descended deep into the dark, leaving behind the mortal coil, she left behind her heaviest burden of all: herself.

Moonlight Fears and Silver Tears

She just stood there with the silver spear in her hand, blood dripping from the tip, standing over the werewolf that had just attacked her family. Just a girl of twelve years with little to no skill in combat, she had just acted on fear. Chest rising and falling with the rhythm of her fast heartbeat, she fought to catch her breath along with her thoughts. Fists clenched tightly over the shaft of the spear, knuckles white, gray eyes searching over the bodies of her mother and father who now both lay motionless feet away from the beast they had fought to protect her from.

The swimming feeling in her head had become overwhelming—it felt like her stomach was rushing up to meet her throat, and it was. Dropping the spear where she stood, she dropped to her knees, catching herself with her hands in the dirt; her body wretched up everything she had eaten for breakfast with her parents. Leaning forward on her knees, Revna coughed and spit what little she had left in her mouth. Staring down at what she just expelled, she was void of any feeling about what she saw before her. All she knew was that at that moment, she no longer had parents to care for her on their little farm just outside the northern village of Hraereksgil.

Getting to her feet, she picked up the heavy silver spear that belonged to her father, carrying it to the small home her mother kept neat and tidy. She set it up against the door in the same place her father would put it after his hunts. Keeping her hand on the shaft of the spear a moment longer than necessary, she closed her eyes, not wanting to return to the massacre lying several feet from the front door.

All she wanted to do was wash up and go lay down in her bed till the next day—dream that everything was okay. No, Revna was a twelve-year-old girl facing reality, forcing herself to be the big girl her mother always encouraged her to be and face her problem head-on. A nightmare really was what she was facing—a horrifying nightmare where she was now an orphan and had to figure out how to survive the coming winter alone.

Feeling the tears flood her eyes as she turned away from her home to walk the distance to her mother's body, she knelt down to take the goddess Hecate's pendant from her neck. The necklace she had worn was covered in her mother's blood and partially stuck in the wound around her neck.

Revna's mother had seen the beast approaching and told her father, who was a hunter, of what Revna knew she thought were just regular animals. Her father got up from the breakfast table to retrieve his spear with a quickness Revna had never seen him use. He didn't have time to don the usual hunting gear he would leave home in for days on end. He had left to meet the werewolf with his spear. He moved like the beast he faced; it was intriguing yet terrifying to witness her father face such a terrifying creature.

Revna's mother, Sybil, pushed her toward the bed she slept in.

"Under! Under!" she shouted.

She wanted so badly to resist her mother's orders to hide. Giving in, Revna slid her body under the wood frame of her single bed.

Sybil rushed back to the window to check on the situation unfolding outside their small farmhouse, her face pale at what she saw. What Revna's father didn't anticipate was that another beast came out of the woods from the east, rushing toward him and hooking his leg with its claws.

Mother had screamed, and that was when Revna heard her open the door and run out of the house to help. Of course, Revna couldn't just stay under the bed. The sheer anxiety of not knowing what was happening was killing her. The screaming of her mother and the shouting of her father had her nerves on end, and the sounds the wolves made gave her skin goose pimples.

Scrambling to get out of her hiding spot, Revna ran to the window to see her mother with her father's spear in hand, trying to stab at the remaining werebeasts. Her father had laid on the ground, struggling to get up after he had sustained multiple wounds. Revna could hear the gurgling sounds of her father choking on his blood as he was failing to hold it all in with his hands. Her mother, crying, tried to kill the beast but had the spear knocked from her hands with a full swipe of the wolf's large paw.

Her eyes widened as she watched her mother get

knocked to the ground, a spray of blood shooting outwards into the air. It was then Revna felt it in her throat—a knot had just welled up inside her.

"Mamma," she whispered.

And it was then she found herself leaving the cottage for the spear that lay several feet back from where her mother had been knocked down, a werewolf over her mother, maw in her neck. It was then Revna had found herself ignored by the wolf, so engulfed in her mother's neck that she shoved the heavy spear into its ribs. The way the silver-inlaid blade just pushed through its flesh like butter made her feel ill as she pushed it in all the way and then pulled it out.

Back to reality, Revna held the necklace of the three moons in the palm of her hand, the silver chain dangling from her small fingers. Pocketing the pendant in her thick brown dress with hand-sewn flowers in some places at the top, now covered in dirt and blood, she stared down at her mother, whose eyes lay open, holding the terror forever in them.

Leaning down, Revna closed her mother's eyes.

"Shh, Mamma. It is now time to rest…"

Moving to her father to do the same, Revna noticed the bodies of the werewolves had changed back to the humans they once were before they were cursed with the disease they carried. Men—they were older men—and it made her feel sick and sad all at once. How could all of this happen to humans? How could something like this affect people in a way that makes them change into animals and attack other people?

Her little mind tried to make all the sense in the world of it, but she just didn't have the knowledge like her father did—nor did she know he had it all. Revna left all the bodies where they lay, herself too weak and small to move them where they had fallen.

Inside the cottage, Revna found the pot of water her mother used to clean her up when she got too dirty. Pouring water from the bucket into it, she gingerly dipped her soiled hands into the water. She watched, against the white of the porcelain bowl, as the water dyed red with the blood from her hands.

Too much in shock from the events of the day, she laid herself in her bed even though it would be several hours before the sun would begin to set. Lying in the bed under the furs of hunted animals brought back by her father, she tucked her head under to hide from the rest of the day.

Closing her eyes as tight as she could, she ignored the pangs of hunger from her stomach as she forced herself to fall asleep. Believing that if she could just go to sleep, maybe everything would be better the next day. Revna felt her heart ache with the notion. Feeling the wetness of her eyes painting her cheeks, she eventually fell asleep to be graced with a dreamless night.

The following day she woke with a horrible pain of hunger as she made the decision not to eat the night before. Sliding out from under her furs, she moved from the back one-bedroom Revna shared with her parents to the cooking stove to find a loaf of bread her mother had left out the day before.

Scavenging for food was something she could do, but how long did she think she could do this for? She knew winter was coming, and she only had so much firewood, so much dried meat.

Sitting at the table like she had the day before, she ate the little bit of food she had found, her nose wrinkling to the stench that was starting to reach the windows from the bodies of the werewolves. Silver from the blade of the spear was working through their veins pretty quickly, making them decompose and change into something quite disgusting.

Leaving her food at the table, she rushed to the windows to shutter them, hoping to keep out the stench. Folding her small hands over her stomach, she felt ill all over again. Turning to slide her little body against the wall, she sat with her knees against her chest. Tears flowed once more down her cheeks, heat rising up to the surface of her skin as she felt her chest heaving.

"Mamma..."

Another day passed, and Revna finally found herself pushing herself to be productive in ways her parents were around the farm. She collected the eggs from the remaining hens for her meals. She made her bed and washed the dishes she dirtied, even covered the bodies of her parents with furs from their bed.

On this particular day, Revna found herself out in the woodpile trying to discern what was dry wood and what was the fresh-cut stuff when a man covered in hunting leathers like her father's—leathers that had an odd symboled patch on the shoulder with bones—appeared.

"Ahem..." The man coughed as he stood feet behind her, trying to mask the concerned look on his face, as he had passed the remaining corpses of werebeast in human form and her parents' bodies. "Excuse me, young lady!"

The sound of his voice made her freeze in place. Her heart began to race. Nothing left her lips as she slowly turned to face the man with her arms full with three logs she believed to be dry enough to burn. Clutching the wood to her chest, she stared at the man, terrified of what would happen next.

Again the man's voice pierced the veil of silence. "I am a friend of your father, Malcum. We often go hunting together." He paused, glancing to the direction where the bodies of her parents lay bloated and starting their decay. "I work with him, and I mean you no harm... Revna? Is that your name? I think I got that right; your father had always spoken about you. Very proud of you, he was."

Taking a step closer to her, he moved slowly, seeing the fear in her gray eyes. "I know what happened here, and I don't think it's best if you stay here alone."

Revna dropped the logs at her feet, the sound of the wood clanking together as they bounced at her feet.

"I tried... Mamma told me to hide... but I couldn't... I had to help."

The man felt his gut clench at her words, knowing the girl of twelve had to pick up a spear and take a life, but he also held a sense of hope for her.

"Come." Holding his hand out to her, he awaited her to take his hand.

Revna didn't hesitate. She rushed in, taking his hand and pushing herself into his torso, wrapping her small arms around him as tightly as she could. Patting her head lightly, he pulled away gently.

"Now, let's pack a few things, Revna. I think it is time for you to come with me to a new home. A place where you can learn to be like your father. To be strong... to kill the very beasts that attacked your parents."

Looking down at the dark-haired girl, he gave his best smile considering the circumstances.

"Well, if that is what you would want?"

Turning her eyes to the bodies of her parents, she knew it was the only way she would be able to honor them— to get revenge.

"Can we burn them first?" she asked, looking up at the man who wore the symbol of the Bone Collectors.

"Well of course, dear child. We are not savages."

The Bone Collector went to work finding her father's ax and cutting down pieces of wood, building a double-wide pyre to burn her mother and father together. While he worked, Revna carefully cleaned her mother and father's bodies of blood and dirt. Wrapping their bodies in white cloth, she had used the rope she had found tied around an old post near the cottage to tie the cloth in place.

That night, Revna and the man who later introduced himself as Renfield burned her parents. While they burned, Revna placed her mother's cleaned pendant around her neck and prayed to her goddess. Renfield packed a bag for the girl while she prayed and cried one last time over the loss of her parents, making sure the silver spear was among her belongings.

"Tomorrow, we leave at dawn. Get some sleep."

Leaving Revna in her bed, sobbing her loss for her

parents, the loss of her home, and for the change that would now come before her, Renfield disappeared to the front room. He looked out the window at the decaying monsters left to rot out in the open. He wouldn't dare allow anyone—even the girl—to bury the bodies, even if the smell got too bad.

A warning they would become, for any of their fellow mates or pack members. And soon, they would have the vengeance of a young warrior on their tails to face.

Glancing back at the curtain that closed the doorway between the front room and the back, Renfield shook his head at the thought but spoke it aloud.

"I am sorry, my dear friend, but she has no other choice."

Several months had passed since that frightful and rightfully awful day for Revna. Now she found herself one of the youngest in training in the organization. The Bone Collectors proved to be a hard and cold organization, run by a small council of men who were hell-bent on the extinction of the werebeast community.

Renfield had presented her to the small council of men three days after they left her childhood home, the only place she had ever known. The men had scrutinized him harshly for his decision, but it was up to Revna to recount the whole situation for them—and how she took up the spear in her own hands, killing the beast as it feasted on her mother's flesh and blood.

As she recounted the whole ordeal without tears, Renfield stood back with others watching, proud of the twelve-year-old who had a heart of steel. After the girl finished her story, the men sat in silence for a moment before they leaned into one another, whispering only enough for themselves to understand. The man in the middle of the group stood up to speak for the whole.

"Revna Vilulf, you have demonstrated a great deal of courage while facing great evil, and we of the council have agreed to allow you to become a Bone Collector."

The man folded his hands down in front of him, crossing his arms to represent crossed bones like that on a pirate's flag. Each of the other men followed suit, bowing their heads for a moment and then looking up to the young girl. Renfield made the same motion behind Revna, and she stood before them unsure of what to do. Crossing her arms, she took a note out of their motions, doing the same—showing respect as she now stood a Bone Collector.

Two years passed. Revna started off her training by servicing the barracks, pulling water from a faraway well and carrying it over her shoulders with two buckets, eventually graduating to wearing weights on her arms and legs. Renfield took personal interest in the girl's training, making every bit of it harder than what the boys went through. He told her over and over that her female body needed harder training than that of the men, and that she needed to become the strongest she could be.

Truth was, her body was much more frail compared to the men, and with that, Renfield wanted her to build her muscle—to be able to fight and tumble with them as equally as she could. Hauling materials most of the time, fighting hand to hand, and training with weapons, Revna grew more and more into a Bone Collector as she grew into a young woman.

It had become known to Renfield that Revna had quite the knack for tracking, a skill her father had taught her as a young child and which had carried on as she got older. They would go out into the woods for exercises, often taking turns finding different students—and every time, she found them. Clearly, it was like a sixth sense she had. She could feel, see, hear, even smell differences in the environment she hunted in.

It was really bizarre—almost inhuman—but it was overlooked by everyone, as she was turning out to be a valued member of their organization.

At the age of sixteen, Revna now stood in her hunting leathers holding the same spear that once belonged to her father. She stood awaiting her orders as she was preparing for her first official hunt as a Bone Collector. Renfield came out of the main building the council members often congregated in. Following suit were two other men.

Stopping before Revna, he looked past her to the four other members that would make up her hunting party.

"Listen up! For the five of you to earn your bones, all of you must be willing to give your lives to the cause! The five of you are tasked with finding the feral werewolf that is terrorizing the village of Kilmire and to eliminate it."

Looking over the five of them, his eyes stopped on Revna, who stood at the head of the party—too eager to get out in the wilderness to prove herself to the organization.

Shifting the spear to the strap upon her back, Revna looked back to her party members, each preparing their weapons of choice for the hunt. Knowing she would be the most likely to find the wolf, she had to fight for one of them to actually listen to her—and that was Lathum.

Lathum became a rival to her. He believed a girl didn't belong in the Bone Collectors and did everything he could to outshine her or make her look bad.

Revna and the four others headed out towards the village of Kilmire, first point being to get started where the attacks kept happening.

"We need to interview the families of the dead and inspect the areas where the beast keeps appearing."

Her words were strong. She knew what she was talking about. She had hunted many other kinds of animals. Nothing she had been training for the past three years could really prepare her for what she was about to get into. Although she had killed the werebeast that was indulging itself in the flesh of her mother, it had been so bloodthirsty it had ignored the girl as it feasted.

It would be foolish of Revna not to admit she was nervous—but she wouldn't let Lathum hear the words leave her lips so long as he was a member of her hunting party. Glancing over at the man who mocked her for being female, who hated the attention she received from the other trainers, she just shook her head.

"I agree!" spoke up one of the other party members as they started their walk towards the village.

Hearing one of the other members of her party agree with her was surprising. Revna thought for sure that it would be a majority of her party against anything she suggested. Shaking away any other negative thoughts that tried to creep into her mind, she pushed onwards with her party to the village.

Kilmire sat two hours away from the major Bone Collector camp where Revna had trained the last three years. It was one of the trading villages they had often visited for supplies and wares for their people. Kilmire had become quite the trading post until it had become threatened with the attacks of werebeasts, which had become much more frequent in the last few months.

Trade started to slow for the village, which wore down the morale of the people who occupied it. Sparsely could anyone be seen outside of their homes or businesses as the group entered the village. Even the once-bustling trading square was quite desolate, except for a smithy working with his apprentice.

Lathum walked near Revna with his hand on the hilt of his sword. He looked around as they entered the town.

"Doesn't look like we will be doing much interviewing."

A smug look crossed his face as he glanced at Revna, as they continued to the side of the village closest to the thick forest that blanketed a large portion of the country between the village and the next.

Ignoring his words, Revna stopped as they reached a section of the village where homes had obviously been lit on fire—where destruction had rained down on families that didn't deserve it. The other four continued to walk towards the destruction, some picking up pieces of wood here and there, and another a half-burned sewn bear.

Ignoring what the others were doing, Revna felt the sudden feeling of panic rise in her chest. Her skin felt hot and tingling all over. Opening and closing her hands, pressing her nails into her palms, she swallowed slowly.

"Don't let them see you like this," she whispered to herself, as she looked up to see where the others were now.

Looking down, she noticed a very large paw print that obviously didn't belong to a domesticated dog or to the average wolf. Sucking in a deep breath, she instantly felt the hunter in her pull forward—taking away the anxiety and panic that had begun to overwhelm her.

Kneeling down, touching the print pressed into the soil, Revna could fit her whole hand into the imprint. Tracing her fingers along the inside of the paw, she then looked up to the sound of a whistle.

"Wow, look at that!"

Lathum knelt next to Revna, touching the paw print—his index finger pointing where one of the largest claws had sunk deep. Stopping with his finger in the soil, he pulled out a piece of mud-covered cloth that had once belonged to someone's clothing.

A seriousness finally slid over the man's face as he looked at the piece of torn cloth and then to Revna, as she looked up from studying the print.

"We have to find this beast and kill it!"

Nodding her head, she looked to the three others who now joined them. Standing to her feet, she pointed towards the forest where the prints casually led, and started walking.

What the group didn't know was that what they thought would be an easy track and kill was really quite the opposite. In fact, they were the ones being hunted.

The five of them had been watched from the moment they left the burned remains of the homes where the beast had attacked some of the villagers—ever since Revna had found the trail in the thick of the forest.

"I don't think this adds up right..." Her words fell on deaf ears as the others stayed further behind her. She lost the trail here and there, and when she found it again, it was in a different place.

Her sixth sense burned and screamed deep within her, leaving her with the urge to reach for the three-mooned necklace that hung hidden under her leather tunic.

The longer they went in circles in the middle of the forest—surrounded by broken branches hung with cloth fragments from dead villagers—the more unease grew. The sun had started to set, though it seemed much darker thanks to the canopy of trees growing so closely together.

"We have been going in a circle!" Revna finally yelled, the sound of her voice sending a bird into the air.

The others stopped to stare at her, leaving Lathum to approach.

"Are you telling me you can't find this beast?"

Shaking her head, she threw her hand to the side. "It's not that I can't find it. It's the mere fact it has lured us into a trap. These tracks have been purposely laid... They must have changed into their human form to hide or sneak out of here..."

Lathum tilted back on his heels a bit, a laugh leaving his throat.

"A bit far-fetched, don't you think?"

A deep, guttural howl ripped the silence away as the group argued about their situation, leaving them wide-eyed in shock.

"Take up your defensive positions!"

Revna held her spear in hand long enough to hear one of her party members scream out, as a dark shadow ripped through the sky, tearing out his throat.

"No! Samuel!" Lathum screamed.

Turning around frantically with his sword in hand, he found himself bumping into another of his group. Without looking, he swung—slicing the underbelly of their archer.

Revna watched as Lathum killed one of their own, his blade tearing through the man in fear.

"Lathum! No!"

The man was filled with fear and anxiety and wasn't thinking clearly. Everything was falling apart, and Revna watched it all happen.

Willard, the other member of their group trying to earn his bones, had his sword drawn. He found the werewolf standing before him, its maw grinning and bloody.

Before he could react, Lathum charged toward the beast, sword pointed at its chest—only to be swatted away like a fly.

Willard felt his pants grow warm as he stared into the wolf's eyes. The beast didn't miss a beat as it walked toward him. Extending its claws, it seemed to laugh under the growling it emitted.

Revna had to keep the rest of her group alive, and Lathum would be no help as he lay motionless six feet away next to the tree he had struck. The smell of copper reached the air as it poured from the open wound on Lathum's unconscious head, and Willard shook like a branch in the wind before the beast that stalked him.

The man stood with his sword wavering back and forth, trying to stand his ground as the beast took off in a near gallop toward him, leaving Revna scared for his life.

The werewolf closed in so fast that all it took was a split-second decision, and her voice rang out as she crashed into Willard.

"Willard! Underbelly!"

Revna ran toward Willard and the beast with her spear in hand, poised to take the beast in the chest as it appeared to float mid-air, launching itself from its rear haunches. Turning toward Revna, nearly overwhelmed, Willard understood as he saw her coming toward him.

Willard dropped flat, pointing his blade upward in time, allowing room for Revna to shove the silver-inlaid blade of her spear into the chest of the massive beast. The searing sound of flesh ripped a painful howl from the creature as it lost momentum, giving the tip of Willard's blade the chance to slice into the soft flesh of its belly.

Blood spilled as the beast fell, knocking the blade from Willard's hands and leaving Revna on the other end of the spear, using gravity and the werebeast's own weight against it. Spinning the creature around just enough, she shoved the blade of her spear deeper into its chest and cranked the handle, twisting the blade.

"You will die for what you've done!"

As she held on to the end of the spear with all her years of strength built up, tears created silver streams down her cheeks in the light of the moon.

The light in the creature's eyes faded into a cloud of

white, and the flesh of the beast changed slowly under the blade of her spear. A mere man hung at the end of her weapon, his flesh still burning under the silver as she pulled it from his chest.

Willard came up beside her with Lathum draped over his arms, holding his head with a free hand.

"You truly belong with the Bone Collectors, Revna."

Lathum's words brought her eyes to meet his own, a look of gratefulness filling them.

"We would all be dead if not for you."

Looking at the blade of her spear, she whispered a prayer to her goddess and nodded to the men left in her party.

"Let's go home."

With that, Revna turned to lead the near-broken men of her party home—to collect their bones.

Springs Warm Embrace

The temperature had to be somewhere in the 20s. The air was absolutely frigid. When the wind blew against the flesh, the cold felt like pins and needles.

It was more bearable for other reasons now than ever, thought Lena. To be alive was a sheer blessing. When the Nebraska winter came, it hit like a wrecking ball. Having been lucky enough to have established safe enough shelter in an old farmhouse, Lena had taken the time to find the materials to reinforce the ground floor's windows and doors.

When she had first arrived at the house, she had been careful to search the premises for the old owners—even other people who might be using the home as a place to live during these times of crisis.

Crisis? Could you even call it that anymore?

A pandemic had smashed into the country like COVID, but it was much harsher than that. It wasn't a lab-disguised or reengineered cold, or whatever the story behind COVID was. No one knew what this virus was. No over-the-counter cold medicine could counter the effects, and the way it spread was abnormal. Many would claim it belonged to the paranormal.

The spread felt straight out of a horror film. Every TV

show and movie ever made about them—you'd think they would've prepared people to handle a situation like this. But it wasn't that simple.

People relied so heavily on the government to tell them how to act, how to react, and what to do in times of crisis. And when the government couldn't come through to help? Chaos.

Lena saw firsthand what happened when the National Guard was deployed—when soldiers started to go AWOL for fear of their own skin and for their families. It was every person for themselves. Pure chaos drove society to the end.

And Lena had no chance of ever making it back to her home.

That was the hardest decision she ever had to make.

The city she lived in was the largest in the state—and also where she had worked at the time when everything hit the fan. That drove her even farther away from home. Cars crowded the streets. People filled the sidewalks. Smoke thickened the air. People were running and screaming, attacking each other.

A familiar scene from every zombie horror film ever made.

It didn't matter what she tried to do. There was nowhere to go with her car. Taking only what was needed, she left the vehicle behind and took to the streets, dodging as many other people as possible. Eventually, she found her way through unfamiliar neighborhoods, staying in houses that people never returned to.

It was rough. She heard "them" outside—bumping into trash cans, setting off car alarms. Lena didn't know if she would ever make it home, but she knew she had to try—for peace of mind.

onths passed, and with them came changing seasons. Fall gave way to winter.

Lena watched the leaves fall from the nearby apple orchard, a place she often scoured for fallen fruit leftover from the harvest. Occasionally, she saw one of "them" out in the fields wandering. It had to be one of the neighbors from the nearby farms.

She had found an old hunting rifle with ammunition in a gun case, along with a hunting crossbow. Keeping the rifle aside for emergencies, Lena practiced with the crossbow in the barn, using bales of hay and wooden targets. With the little experience she had, she trained herself.

When she found old wood and tools in the barn, Lena worked at boarding up the windows flush with the farmhouse's wraparound porch. In the evenings, she stayed on the second floor with minimal light—out of paranoia that someone would eventually notice she was there and try to take what she had.

Over time, she made trips on foot to nearby houses in search of supplies. Knowing Nebraska winters could be mild or extreme, she only took what she needed.

The hardest part was transporting her finds.

Eventually, she discovered a neighboring farm with horses still in the stables. Untouched.

She had some knowledge of horses from her time volunteering with a horse therapy organization. Testing the temperaments of each animal, she gave them rubdowns and proper feedings after so long without care. Observing what little they'd eaten from leftover hay, Lena freed all the horses—except one.

She saddled a red-brown mare and brought her back to the barn at the farmhouse, now her safehouse. Securing the barn and feeding and watering the mare, Lena whispered:

"I can't lose the only friendly face I've found since the start of this mess." Her words fell upon empty air as she shook the barn doors to make sure they were tightly shut from the outside.

Next, she needed to find something the horse could reasonably pull. She thought she'd seen a single-horse cart at one of the other farms and made a mental note.

It had begun to get dark. And with the dark came the unknown. With the mare secure, Lena returned to the farmhouse. Stepping through the front door on the wraparound porch, she entered a room she had repurposed for storage and organization.

She had placed totes she'd found throughout the house around the room, moving the heaviest furniture in front of the boarded-up windows. The center of the room was left open for her latest project.

In the cellar, Lena had found bins filled with family belongings—items she carefully sorted into piles, checking each one for anything of use. Since the beginning of it all, her mind had shifted straight into survival mode. Everything she'd learned from her time in the service and beyond had kicked into high gear.

She knew it wasn't safe yet to try and enter the city without a plan. Being alone made it even harder.

Going through the house inch by inch, she searched for anything that could aid in her survival. It consumed most of her time—but it was also a reprieve from the constant thoughts about her family.

Worry had set in, as it should.

Lena was a mother of three. At the time when everything had begun, the children would've been going home with the help of their older sister. Her husband would've been home to greet them.

Hope—blind and unwavering—kept her going. Hope that her husband, Jared, had gotten them to safety.

Looking over every one of the bins, Lena had them organized by item: batteries, lanterns, canned goods. She yawned and moved toward the kitchen, where the old gas stove still worked.

Cracking open a can of beans, she set them to warm on the burner. Watching the bubbles rise, she pulled the pot off the heat and ate straight from it with a spoon.

"I need to sleep. Tomorrow I must haul in wood for the stove."

She shrugged and laughed to herself at the sound of her own voice—talking aloud to no one.

After promptly cleaning her dish, Lena retired to the bedroom upstairs off the kitchen. A large bed filled with blankets awaited her.

Without the convenience of a weather station or television, Lena woke to a white dusting over the ground. Standing at the window that overlooked the front of the farmland, she let out a long sigh.

"Imagine when we used to complain about it… Now there are real reasons to complain."

Letting out a soft laugh, she reached up to wipe a single tear trailing down her cheek.

Pulling on her worn jeans, she found a pair of old coveralls—obviously too large—but held them in her hands anyway. She kept the rifle and crossbow in her room at night, moving them around the farm with her during the day.

Dressed in the oversized coveralls for warmth, Lena relied on the stove only at night to preserve resources. Slipping her feet into her boots, she slung the rifle over her shoulder and secured the crossbow across her back.

She retreated to the main floor, stored the rifle safely in the pantry, then headed outside to check on the mare in the barn.

Each morning, she completed her self-assigned chores one by one. After finishing the first few, she re-entered the house and ate from a jar of canned peaches she'd found in the pantry.

"I am afraid I may have to start venturing into the city for supplies…"

Letting out a sigh, Lena peered through the back kitchen window overlooking the barren farmland. In the distance, she could just make out the outline of the city.

A pit opened in her stomach—sick and anxious all at once. No amount of preparation made the feeling any better.

She stirred the last few peaches in the can with her fork, finished the fruit, rinsed the utensil in the sink, and left the can for later.

Lena knew she had to inspect the houses closest to the

city limits. She needed to find a place to leave her horse. It wasn't safe to bring the mare into the city. She feared losing her—her only companion and her only mode of transport that didn't rely on gasoline.

Packing a bottle of water in her coverall pocket and grabbing her gloves, Lena left the house and returned to the barn.

She saddled the mare she'd so carefully cared for throughout the winter. Reaching up to the saddle horn and placing her foot in the stirrup, Lena swung herself up in one fluid motion. Shifting into position, she settled in to ride out toward the city.

Several hours passed as Lena traveled house to house, moving miles closer to the outskirts of civilization. One stop yielded an old army rucksack—and a bit of rest for the mare.

After brushing down the horse to give her back a break, Lena offered water and hay found in another barn. Scratching the mare's neck, she looked toward the city.

The pit in her stomach grew.

Once rested, she remounted and continued forward. The closer they got to the city, the more cars—and the more death—she saw. Burned bodies lay inside the skeletons of vehicles. Some had been decimated by the military's efforts to stop the undead. Whatever lives they'd once had had melted away.

Staying to the side of the road, Lena guided the mare as the gravel turned to pavement. Ahead, she saw a small cluster of houses forming their own mini neighborhood just outside the city—waiting to be consumed by the growing monster.

Some of the homes had large fenced areas—once meant for goats or maybe a horse or two. That meant one of them might have a stable where she could leave her mare safely.

Checking her wristwatch, she saw the sun would set soon—and with it, the temperature would plummet. She squeezed the mare with her legs and leaned in slightly. The horse galloped forward.

A few miles out, Lena slowed the mare. Several cars were parked in and around the area. It wasn't as safe as she'd hoped.

She spotted one house with a stable and an outdoor arena and led the mare toward it, keeping distance from the parked vehicles.

"Good girl."

Leaning forward, she patted the mare's thick neck as they came up behind the chosen house. Sliding the crossbow from her back, she flicked the safety off one-handed while directing the horse toward the arena.

Scanning the grounds for movement—anything human or otherwise—Lena's heart pounded.

As they rounded the side of the house, she realized she'd been holding her breath. But nothing stirred.

She exhaled and reset the safety on the crossbow, then slid down from the saddle.

"Come."

She led the mare into the arena and let her roam freely inside the fencing. It was time to clear the house.

With the crossbow in hand, Lena walked toward the front of the house. Parked in the drive were a truck and two sedans. One of the sedans had its doors hanging open. The others looked like they belonged to the residents.

A wave of hot and cold washed over her body as she reached the door. Her gut twisted.

She hovered her hand near the handle of the dark-blue door, its paint a striking contrast to the slate-gray house. There was a smudge of dried blood on the wood near the brass handle.

Lena knew it wouldn't be pretty inside.

Sucking in a deep breath, she gripped the handle and brought the crossbow up into both hands, ready to shoot. As the door opened, it bounced off the back wall. She caught it with her foot and paused.

The inside was dark, save for the light that filtered through the uncovered windows. The house smelled of stale air and rot.

Trying not to cough, Lena bent her head to breathe lower to the ground. While still bent, she heard rustling behind the couch.

As she looked up, a small figure slowly rose from the floor.

A gurgling sound came from the child's throat—or what was left of it. There was a gaping hole where her neck should've been.

Nausea swelled in Lena's stomach, rising with every mile of dread she'd carried toward the city.

She froze.

The girl's matted hair was caked with old blood. Her

pajamas were torn at the neck and shoulders.

A whisper left Lena's lips. "Forgive me."

She raised the crossbow and pulled the trigger.

The bolt struck the girl in the forehead, her head jerking back in a single motion. Her small body fell with a thump behind the couch.

The sound roused something further down the hallway. A door began to rattle under the force of repeated impact.

There was no time to think.

Pinching the crossbow between her knees, Lena rewound the string and loaded another bolt. She raised it just in time to see another zombie round the corner from the back bedrooms.

This one was faster—and already damaged.

Lena sidestepped into the living room, trying to keep the couch between her and the creature. She took aim, but her foot caught on a toy she hadn't seen.

The bolt fired wide, missing entirely.

Panic shot through her. Backpedaling toward the wall, she struggled to reload as the zombie tripped over an end table lunging for her. The banging from the bedroom door behind them grew louder.

Finally, the bolt clicked into place.

The creature reached for her.

Lena pulled the trigger. The body dropped just feet from her.

Her heart pounded in her temples. A dizzy rush overtook her.

"Not now... can't be passing out."

She breathed in and out, steadying herself.

Blinking a few times, she knelt and braced one foot against the skull of the zombie. With a firm tug, she pulled the bolt free.

Wiping it on the tattered remains of the body, she prepared another shot and moved around the couch to retrieve the first bolt.

At the end of the hallway, the rattling door thudded with each strike. Low, hungry moans echoed behind it.

"Yes, yes... I hear you."

She glanced at the other rooms. A door to the left—a bedroom. To the right, likely a bathroom. She didn't know where the other zombie had come from.

She'd have to clear them all.

Standing over the second zombie—the one that had occupied the last room at the end of the hall—Lena concentrated on slowing her breath. She leaned down and yanked the bolt from its skull.

The house was cleared.

One by one, she dragged the bodies outside. The ground was too frozen to dig graves, so she left them out of sight behind the house—away from the arena, where the mare couldn't see them.

After clearing the barn, she safely stabled the horse for the night. Tomorrow, she would begin the trek into the city.

The cold of winter had slowed the dead. Something about the freezing temperatures dulled their movement. It was hard to explain without the science, but every corpse she'd encountered near the farmhouse had been sluggish— barely mobile.

It gave her hope that she might survive the city.

But it wasn't just the dead she had to look out for.

Lena hadn't had human contact since the day everything fell apart. The day it truly became every man, woman, and child for themselves.

She'd gone over hundreds of scenarios in her mind—what she'd say, what she'd do, how to act. But reality never unfolded the way you imagined it would.

Standing at the front door of the cleared house, lost in thought, Lena looked toward the stable where her mare happily ate hay. Tomorrow, she'd give her everything she had—and hope it would be enough.

She was about to risk everything to return to the place she'd once called home.

How far would she get before it all went bad?

Pushing through the doorway and closing the screen door behind her, Lena locked the door tight. Leaning against it, she let out a deep breath.

"Well... time to see what's left in this place."

She'd already skimmed the cupboards before taking the horse to the barn. There were a few canned goods and jars of pickled items. She found the can opener and cracked open a can of cold beans and weenies.

Dinner of champions.

Lena flopped onto the couch, her crossbow resting across her belly. She fell asleep faster than expected after the day's exploits.

ebraska winters were unpredictable. One day could be brutally cold, the next deceptively mild.

Lena woke early and began her journey into the city. Crossbow in hand, safety off, she was ready to shoot.

The interstate, where she'd abandoned her car long ago, was a graveyard. Some vehicles were still filled with the dead. Others were just empty shells—burned, melted, hollow.

Cautiously, she wove around them, peeking into windows and popping open trunks, searching for anything useful—leftover supplies, groceries, tools. More often than not, she came up empty-handed.

But occasionally, she struck gold. A handgun in one car, with a single loaded magazine.

Looking up at the sky, she noticed it was clearer than usual. No hazy gray clouds. And warmer.

"This might pose a bit of a problem..."

But it was too late to turn back.

She had already passed the interstate and entered the local streets crowded with tall buildings. Was it still winter? She wasn't sure anymore. Time had slipped away from her. Survival had stolen her calendar.

"To think about it... it really has been getting warmer..."

Turning a corner, she stopped short.

A massive group of the undead stood ahead, swaying in place. They hadn't seen her yet.

Lena froze.

One wrong sound could mean death.

Could they move fast again now that the cold

was lifting?

Slowly, carefully, she backed away—quiet as possible.

Then her foot struck a glass bottle. It clinked and spun across the pavement.

Two of the undead turned their heads, twitching like lizards, sharp with curiosity. Their shoulders shifted. Their heads tilted.

Their eyes met hers.

Lena exhaled the breath she'd been holding and bolted.

"Not today!"

She sprinted in the opposite direction—one she had intentionally avoided earlier.

The streets were choked with debris. Garbage. Burned-out vehicles. A child's stroller lay on its side.

Everything she saw painted a picture of chaos. The chaos that had shattered the world.

Her calves burned. It hurt to keep going. But when she looked back, she saw them gaining.

The warming spring had reanimated the dead.

She hadn't misjudged the city—she'd misjudged the weather.

Block after block, Lena ran.

Turning a corner, she found another group of undead in a dormant state—like hibernation. She ducked behind a dumpster, trying to catch her breath and slow her thundering heart.

But the sound of her body slamming against the rusting metal echoed too loudly.

"Shit."

Some of the nearby undead stirred. The group she'd fled had caught up, their moans rising in pitch as they pressed forward. She scanned the surrounding buildings, desperate for any escape.

Spying a metal door hanging ajar, she launched herself toward it, shoving it open and diving inside.

She slammed the exit-only door shut behind her just as a wave of bodies crashed against it.

The groaning on the other side was immediate, relentless. The door vibrated under the weight of the undead. They pounded against it—hungry, angry, and reawakened.

Inside, it was pitch black.

Lena hadn't thought about where she was going, only that she had to get away. Now she leaned against the cool metal of the door, catching her breath, her body trembling.

Her heart beat in her throat. Her head pounded.

"Shit," she whispered again.

She was trapped in an unknown building with only one exit—and dozens of bodies between her and it.

Her eyes slowly adjusted.

Shelving units surrounded her, some tipped over, boxes torn open. A clothing store. The shadows of mannequins and wrecked displays surrounded her.

Fear prickled across her skin. She had felt safer outside—even in the house she had cleared on the edge of the city.

Here, in the dark, she was blind. Alone. Exposed.

Was being alone her downfall? Had her distrust, her need to do everything on her own, brought her to this?

As she moved forward, she passed glass cases—

smashed and empty. Jewelry once housed inside glimmered faintly through dirt-smudged windows.

She leaned over a counter, catching her breath.

Behind her, a piece of broken glass crunched.

She turned in time to see a dead woman, jaw slack, reaching out.

A hand grabbed Lena's coat, yanking her toward a mouth full of blackened teeth. Lena screamed, startled by the strength of the decomposing body.

She raised her crossbow one-handed, aiming at the head, but stumbled backward over a fallen clothes rack. The bolt missed.

The zombie pulled harder with both hands.

Lena scrambled, pushing with her legs to get away. The crossbow hung uselessly at her side.

She reached for anything to fight with—anything to smash or stab.

The pistol!

She fumbled into her pocket, fingers closing around the grip. No time for the safety.

She pressed the muzzle to the woman's skull and pulled the trigger.

The bang exploded in her ears. The woman dropped, her body limp.

Warm gore splattered her face. Some landed on her lips.

She gagged and retched, rolling to the side.

As she pushed the body off, another pair of arms wrapped around her.

She didn't scream this time.

Fingers groped her body strangely, unnaturally. A mouth latched onto her neck, and pain burned through her shoulder.

Another one.

And behind that, more—tripping over each other, hungry after months without prey.

"This is some bullshit."

She raised the pistol and fired again, killing the one on top of her. Her ears rang louder than ever. The window glass shattered.

More poured in.

This was supposed to be a safe trip. A calculated return. A risk carefully weighed against the cold of winter.

But spring had come early. And Lena hadn't known.

She didn't know that the temperature would drop again in just a few days—freezing the world once more. She didn't know that survival had been just within reach.

As more and more of them clawed toward her, Lena accepted her fate and just laughed—a sound born of exhaustion and disbelief— as more and more came to embrace her at last.

The Hive

The city was large, futuristic, and industrial—it was like a monster that loomed over the human race. Looking up was disorienting, with cars flying overhead and towering buildings that climbed so high they disappeared into the clouds themselves.

On the surface, the city was old, worn out, and tired. Some parts were poorer than others. Wood was a building material of the past; metal gleamed all the way into the skies while rusted closely to the earth's crust. Lights decorated the buildings in all colors—some flashing signs advertising exotic services, others warning air traffic above that buildings were present.

Skywalks extended from some buildings here and there, mostly corporate headquarters of high importance and multiple hospitals. Science had taken off in directions the imagination could barely fathom. Technology had become the new religion of the people.

No one truly believed in death anymore. Even the very mention of it brought laughter to those who could afford the pieces often seen sewn into the sides of their heads.

With the great progression of time and science, it was

also clear that nothing would ever change about the greed of the upper class. Those with deep pockets still controlled the government. They still decided who would receive upgrades, who would get what when it came to human enhancement.

Unlike them, Asya worked hard to fight against the status quo. She wanted to bring upgrades to the lower classes. Why should the rich be the only ones allowed such amazing healthcare—and the ability to prolong their lives?

Asya had served her world honorably in the many world wars fought across the universe, earning her multiple titles. Being a part of the world's military came with certain privileges, like replacement limbs when yours were blown to pieces.

Asya had earned herself a new arm and some head tech during her time in service. It gave her a step up from the lower classes—and a dose of pity from the upper ones whenever they saw her.

She had earned her gear. But again, she was looked down on for where she chose to live after being discharged with honorable mention.

Instead of taking a seat among the high-rollers, she returned to the surface—among the other bottom feeders. She salvaged tech the rich threw out, upgrades they considered "outdated," and saved them for those who couldn't afford anything else.

It was a day like any other for Asya: bent over a pile of parts, sifting through them one by one. Occasionally, she tossed a piece into a black box to her left. A loud would echo as each part hit the side before sliding down to join the others.

She never looked at where she threw the pieces. It didn't matter. In time, they would all end up under a large magnifying glass, surrounded by mechanical tools for repair.

The sound of electronic chimes echoed as the rusted door of her shop opened and slammed shut. A male voice called out from behind her.

"Always neck deep in body parts!"

A snicker left her lips. She leaned back onto her heels, turning her slightly grease-smudged face toward the man.

"Cyrus, what brings you to the ol' Rusty Hinge?"

Standing up, Asya moved to the counter to grab a greasy rag and casually wiped her fingers as Cyrus stepped inside. The large, bulky man—easily six foot two—leaned over the counter with a grin.

As she leaned in, she caught the scent of old tobacco... and something else she couldn't quite place.

"What is it, Cyrus? What you got for me?"

Usually, when the big man came into her shop, he had some sort of information to sell. Anything he shared came with strings attached.

Meeting his deep blue eyes, she shook her head and pushed off the counter, turning to walk away.

The man was all about suspense.

He threw his hands into the air. "Okay! Okay!"

Rolling her eyes, she sighed. "I really don't have time for your games today. I've got customers to fix and very few parts to do it with. The fly-highs are keeping a lot to themselves these days—their dumps have been less and less."

Folding her arms over her chest, she felt the weight of

tools pressing into her from the apron's front pockets.

Cyrus leaned into the counter again and twitched his index finger, motioning for her to come closer.

She rolled her eyes again but stepped toward him.

"I hear a large shipment of new parts will be flying low overhead in about a week's time," he said. "And I know a few people looking to split the earnings…"

Eyes wide, Asya pretended to be shocked by his proposal. Silence fell between them.

"Cyrus, do you know how traceable those parts are?"

Watching the man push off the counter, she saw the excitement bubbling beneath his tattooed skin.

"That's the thing, Asya! This is stuff that hasn't yet been numbered. Stuff that has yet to be…"

He stuttered over the last words, but she knew what he meant. If done correctly, it could be a true gift to the sick and forgotten—those who walked the earth, dragging broken bodies behind them.

"Look, Cyrus. Give me a night to think more about this. Do you have a crew to pull it off?"

He nodded furiously.

She brought her thumb and index finger to her chin in thought. "Well. Be off with yourself and come back tomorrow evening around closing. I'll have an answer for you."

As Cyrus exited the shop, he barely dodged the small figure of a young girl stepping through the front door.

"Asya!"

The squeaky voice echoed across the Rusty Hinge.

A girl with fiery red hair stood with one metal leg cocked awkwardly to the side.

"Mae, what brings you in?"

Asya started toward her. Mae stepped forward, but her prosthetic locked up with a horrible grinding sound.

As the girl lost balance, Asya rushed in and lowered her carefully to the floor.

"What have I told you about this leg? You need to take care of it the best you can. I still haven't found or received the necessary parts to give you an upgrade."

She shook her head and tapped her tongue against her teeth in a motherly .

"I know, I know!"

Crossing her arms, Mae watched as Asya retrieved an oil can and began working on the locked joint.

"Now! Be on your way. I must close up."

As Mae stood, Asya smiled with her lips—but her eyes held a quiet sadness.

Every night, Mae made it a routine to visit Asya. Sometimes she asked about inventory. Other times, when she felt she was being a bother, she brought small gifts she found while digging through the streets.

Following the girl to the door, Asya caught it behind her.

"Now, Mae. Please take care and give it a rest. I'll let you know when I get the parts in to fix you up—just like everyone else I've got on my list."

Mae paused and looked over her shoulder with a smile, then disappeared into the dark streets.

Asya closed the door behind her, turned the locks, reached up to slide the bolt into the ceiling, then stomped the floor bolt into place.

"That girl," she said softly, resting her back against the door. "She is persistent."

Closing her eyes, she allowed her breath to slow to the pounding rhythm of her heartbeat.

The night went quicker than Asya imagined, which she was thankful for. Plagued with nightmares of her time in the service, a peaceful night of rest hardly ever graced her.

She was up before the rise of the sun—though the sun was most often blocked by the massive buildings that rose so high no one on the surface of the earth could ever see their tops. Stories spread like old wives' tales among the children of the surface, claiming the buildings grew on their own. Many of them were run by AI and other technologies.

Reflective solar veils could be seen plastered to the sides of these towers, meant to help bring the rays of sun closer to the poor below. Though it didn't help much—people still suffered from vitamin D deficiencies.

More often than not, Asya found herself among those who had to take a cocktail of vitamins just to survive on the surface. Unlike others, she got hers free from the government due to her status.

Feeling the pills slide down her throat, chased by a sip of cool water, she checked the time through the augmented reality screen in the lens of her right eye. Just a thought—and the display faded away.

With a yawn, she set the cup down on the old worn sink in her bathroom.

"Looking rough."

She stared at herself in the mirror and reached for the rubber band she used to pull her long black and orange dreads into a ponytail.

She was already dressed for the day—nothing fancy, just her usual coveralls and boots.

Opening the shop was the same song and dance as always, sometimes with a regular customer waiting just outside the door.

Typical repairs on fully augmented body parts. Minor adjustments for new recipients. Asya was always busy—even if that didn't mean face-to-face encounters.

Several hours passed with Asya digging through the box of parts she'd worked on the night before. Finally, she reached the bottom.

"All of that and little of what I need."

She examined a small chip between her fingertips and tossed it into the "keep" pile—which was much smaller than the "trash" pile.

Letting out a deep sigh, she heard the door alarm chime—the warning that someone had entered the shop.

Dusting herself off and turning to meet the customer, she saw Cyrus and two others.

Checking the time, she looked at the door. "Mind locking it behind yourselves so no one else comes in to catch our conversation?"

The smallest of the three men turned and bolted the door as Cyrus and the medium-built man approached her counter.

"So, Asya. How was your sleep? Got an answer for us?"

Stepping closer, she pulled a well-worn stool toward her and sat, clasping her hands together.

"Who's your business partners? I wasn't aware you would bring company to our meeting."

The shorter man joined them. He had green eyes and long hair tied back in a greasy ponytail.

Cyrus gestured back toward the two men standing silently beside him. "These two are the ones who'll be helping me acquire the goods. They're the ones very interested in supplying you, Gear-head."

Leaning back, Cyrus folded his bulky arms across his chest.

"They know of your exploits in the world's wars. And the good you do down here on the surface."

Looking between the two men, he gave a short snort.

"They're investors in your work—in keeping you in business, so to speak."

Staring each man down, Asya released her clasped hands and pointed at them, one after the other.

"Interested investors? Ha!"

A loud guffaw escaped her lips. She stood and walked around the counter, her eyes never leaving the pair. They turned to follow her with their own.

"And what strings are attached to these investments?"

Asya knew there were always strings. Always a catch.

The taller, medium-built man stepped forward. Asya noted his tasteful clothing for someone walking the surface. He clearly had a taste for sky life and likely spent his money on the finest things.

"Please, we really don't mean to have any sort of 'strings' or 'wrongdoing' added to this. We truly want to support your business and, well..."

He reached into his jacket.

Asya immediately backed up, her face hardening.

"What are you doing??"

"Please—it's just my wallet."

He held it up and pulled out a photograph: a small girl with a prosthetic that looked... familiar.

"See? This is my little sister. You helped her when my mother couldn't. When I couldn't."

Cyrus stepped up between Asya and the man.

"What Oscar is saying," Cyrus said, "is that they want to help you—and support you politically, too. The government is trying to keep the middle class and the poor from receiving the same care as the sky people. And you're allowing them— us—to live."

Silence fell between the four of them.

Asya weighed everything carefully. Her intuition screamed at her to believe them. To trust them.

Breaking the long and awkward silence, she looked each man in the eyes.

"Let's do this. I just need to know—how are the parts going to get to me?"

The two men with Cyrus smiled. The shortest one spoke up.

"We have a network of children and other folks on the surface who'll collect the pieces as they rain down. Over time, they'll make their way back to the Hive. You."

A laugh burst from Cyrus.

"See? They're bees collecting our pollen to make the honey."

The Hive spent several days planning how they were going to attack the shipment of high-tech cybernetic parts meant for the upper-class sky people. Carefully changing their meeting locations and using archaic methods of communication—ones thought to be of "ancient" times—they soon developed what they believed to be a solid plan.

It was late in the evening, and the four of them sat around a table drinking their choice of beverage, discussing pieces of the plan.

"I want it to be clear." Asya slapped her hand lightly on the tabletop to get the attention of the three men who meant to pull this off at all costs. "I don't want any casualties. Avoid death at all costs."

Each of the men took turns looking at one another. The silence between them was palpable.

The green-eyed man, Clive, spoke up. "Asya, what you ask of us may not be avoidable. What we've learned is that the airship will have a small crew to fly it—but also a squad of six trained guards."

Resting his hands on the table, clasped together in a manner so relaxed it irritated Asya, he continued. "We may have to inflict some sort of damage…"

The look on her face disappeared. How could she ask these men to go into this mission without the intent to kill? She knew perfectly well they would be armed—and that some of them might come out wounded.

"I just ask that no one is killed on purpose. If you have

to do it in self-defense…"

A sigh left her lips.

"It is what it is."

Standing from the table, her hand lifted, leaving only the tips of her metal fingers lingering on the surface.

"This is where I leave you, gentlemen. Tomorrow, we will complete our mission with success—and I mean this without a doubt."

A loud chuckle left Cyrus. "Quite the optimist."

Turning to give him a look, Asya took her leave.

The most anticipated day had come, and it didn't arrive alone. Anxiety ached in the back of Asya's mind as she ran the shop like any normal business day, keeping up appearances.

She conducted a few minor surgeries and sold some medicine she had on hand. But the later it got, the more the knot in her stomach grew.

With closing time in sight, she had already prepared her dinner and was eating behind the counter of her shop when the sound of a very familiar guest filled the room.

In mid-bite, Asya held the fork just before her lips, eyes lifting to meet the glow of light catching on the fiery red hair of Mae.

"Asya!"

Looking at the time, then at the girl, she frowned slightly. "Mae, don't you have something better to do than constantly check in here for parts?"

Mae brought her hands to her hips, elbows bent, and laughed loudly.

"No!"

Dropping her hands, she moved forward as quickly as her pieced-together cybernetic leg allowed. At the counter, Mae pulled herself up by the glass.

"Asya, I will always be a customer—even when I'm not able to get what I need. I have faith that you will fix me soon."

Smiling, Asya finally took the bite that had grown cold on her fork. The child turned and left the shop as quickly as she'd entered, always leaving Asya just as perplexed about her as ever.

Locking up gave Asya a moment to rest before the big event. The closer it came, the larger the knot inside her grew. At this point, it felt like she was growing a cable in her gut. Her whole body felt electric.

It brought back the same feelings she'd experienced during her army years—the moments just before battle when her companions would psych themselves up.

But Asya didn't do that ritual this time.

No. She wanted this mission to be as peaceful as possible.

With the front of the shop locked up, Asya disappeared into her personal apartment to dress in clothing she hadn't worn in many years.

Tactical pants in black. A gray tank top with a jacket overtop. She secured her dreads tightly back.

No lethal weapons were strapped to her body—only a retractable stun baton. Nothing like a little shock for those who dared get in her way.

ater that evening, Asya met up with the other three. Each was dressed in their attire of choice, prepared for whatever the ship's guards might throw at them.

"Now, let's get into our room at Cloud 9 Hotel," Cyrus stated. "I booked us the room just above where the ship will be flying by on its route—as it begins the slow ascent toward the cybernetics port."

Oscar stepped closer to Asya.

"Why are they flying so low, anyway?"

Smirking, Asya folded her arms.

"They believe it's safer to fly between the buildings. They think it'll keep air pirates from connecting their ships and stealing the merchandise."

As she spoke, a wide, shit-eating grin spread across Cyrus's face.

The three men watched Asya disappear farther into the empty alleyway where they'd met twenty minutes earlier. Taking a quiet moment to admire the woman they idolized, they quickly moved to catch up—following her lead as she guided them toward the hotel.

Fifty floors up into the hotel, they had booked the room—and it wasn't luck that landed them the perfect location either.

The men had a connection with the hotel manager, being AI and all. They got what they wanted. In fact, they had paid for the entire floor to remain closed and off-limits. The elevator skipped it altogether with help from the AI host, and the stairwell access door stayed locked—except for the crew, who had special keycards.

Under the disguise of the floor being "under repairs," the crew entered the room facing the north side of the building.

With Oscar leading the group inside, he let out a hoot at the sight of the supplies they'd carefully listed out for their AI friend to gather. Every item was stacked neatly against the back wall of the room near the windows.

Cyrus pushed past Clive and Oscar to get to the gear first, his hands practically itching.

Rolling her eyes, Asya closed the door behind her, despite the floor being locked down from prying eyes.

"Now, now, gentlemen. Quit drooling—you'll ruin the gear."

A soft chuckle escaped her lips, catching the men off guard. They froze, then looked at one another in shock. The moment passed quickly, and they joined in the laughter.

For the first time, they heard the great Gearhead laugh.

"You can laugh?" Oscar said as he moved toward the box containing the gravity boots—boots designed to keep them glued to the ship's hull when they made the great leap.

Ignoring the comment, Asya stepped over to take a pair in her size and began pulling them on.

"I suggest getting your boots on and getting the windows open. Sky will mask the openings with their holograms. When the ship's directly beneath us, we deploy."

She zipped the inner linings and locked them into place, tucking her own boots under the couch where she'd sat to put on the new gear.

With the others following her lead, she stood to

continue preparing the room for the heist—one that could supply every soul on the surface with a chance at new cybernetics to replace failing body parts.

Opening the large windows that led to a small balcony, the team heard the soft puttering of the airship as it rounded the buildings—carefully navigating the lower city to protect itself.

Turning to meet the eyes of each of her teammates, Asya pointed downward at the ship just now coming into range.

Blending into the dark, the four of them moved to the edge of the platform, preparing to jump.

A massive airship made of penny copper with sails of gold and black sailed between Cloud Nine Hotel and the buildings across from it. The bubble dome of its hull held porthole windows and a few hatches for venting steam.

One by one, each team member jumped from the ledge without hesitation. The gravity boots activated, locking them onto the ship's material like fresh hardware.

Inside the ship, only faint pangs of impact could be heard—quickly lost under the roar of the engines as they devoured minerals mined from the great asteroid belt near the planet.

Asya crept close to the ship's body, leading the others to the underbelly. She pointed to a hatch often used by mechanics to access areas near the fuel reserves.

Hanging upside down, masked by the darkness of night, Clive took over the entry process.

He noticed the soft glow of a green pad and connected a small device from his wrist, a cable spooling out with a click. Muttering a few strange commands, the hatch's panel turned blue with a soft hum, and the door clicked open.

Clive reached for the long handle, pulled it across, and unlatched the hatch. Looking back at Asya and the others, he pulled himself in and clicked his heels together—disengaging his boots.

One by one, the others followed, clicking their heels and slipping inside—each body disappearing from view. Clive slowly closed the hatch behind them, sealing it tight to avoid triggering alarms.

Asya turned to her wrist and pulled up a holographic map of the ship. She pointed with her free hand.

"Here," she said in a low tone.

She looked toward a door just three feet in front of them.

"Through that door, we take a left into the cargo hold. We should find all the crates marked with a sword and shield. Those are the parts we'll drop to the bees."

Each of them made eye contact, acknowledging silently that now it was time to get down and dirty.

The knot in Asya's stomach grew tighter.

Adrenaline surged through her veins as she let Cyrus lead the way—not just because he was the largest of the four, but because he fancied himself the bruiser. He wanted to take the first blow from whatever guards they might encounter.

And Asya was happy to let him.

They made her out to be a warrior, and yes—she had been one. But she wasn't eager to jump into conflict the way some of her companions were.

After everything she had witnessed while serving her

world, peace was all she wanted to know. Peace was all she wanted her species to know—and everyone she met.

True equality might have been a fantasy told to the children of her planet, but Asya still believed in it. And she was willing to fight for it.

Cyrus was the first through the door, following the hall without any issue—not a soul in sight, as it were.

Silently, the crew crept through the corridor, a long narrow hallway that branched into three directions. Hearing voices coming from the corridor to the right, Cyrus reached back with his right hand and motioned for the others to duck low against the wall.

Reaching into his pocket, he pulled out a brutal-looking pair of brass knuckles—oddly perfect for his massive hand. He flexed his fingers into a fist and out again, preparing to meet the guard rounding the corner—one about to be relieved of far more than his post.

The guard, dressed in dark blue coveralls, turned the corner and was met by a large open palm that clamped over the lower half of his face, followed by a quick, crushing blow to the gut delivered by Cyrus's metal-laced knuckles. The air whooshed from the man's lungs.

Cyrus caught him as he slumped, easing the unconscious guard silently to the floor.

He looked back for Asya's approval, then checked both adjacent corridors for other threats. At her signal, the team followed. Asya was sandwiched between the men—Oscar in the rear, Clive just ahead.

Taking the left corridor, the group paused outside a door, muffled voices audible from within. Cyrus waited for it to open. It didn't. They moved on.

At last, they reached the door leading to the cargo hold. Sliding past Cyrus, Clive pulled out his magical cord and got to work on the keypad.

Oscar turned his back to Asya's, watching the way they'd come. Asya pressed her metal hand to the wall, feeling for any vibration or shift within the ship.

A blue light blinked on the panel, and Clive slipped silently through the door. From within, the sounds of a struggle echoed.

Cyrus was through next. He found Clive already holding a guard in a chokehold, carefully lowering him to the floor.

Asya slipped past them and leaned over the railing. Below, the hold stretched out—rows of chained-down crates, each marked with a sword and shield. Their target.

Without a word, she motioned for the men to take their rehearsed positions. The plan was in motion.

They moved in search of other guards. Asya descended into the hold, taking quick mental inventory.

Oscar appeared beside her and whispered, "I think the room we passed was a lounge. The other guards aren't here."

The other two joined them shortly.

"Let's get these out the bottom hatch quickly before we have any more trouble."

Clive started work opening the lower hatch while the others moved crates into place.

Grinning, Asya pried the lids open with her mechanical arm—revealing pristine cybernetic parts, gleaming and untouched.

A gust of wind whistled through the room as the hatch opened fully. The sound faded, leaving only the rushing air below.

Asya stepped to the edge and looked down through the gaping hole at the city beneath them.

Small golden lights dotted the surface—bees in place to receive their pollen.

Clive and Oscar tipped one of the crates, spilling parts through the hatch. One by one, they emptied each crate until only a single one remained.

"I suggest you guys start departing," Asya said with a smile. "We need to get out before they discover what we've done."

Cyrus gripped her shoulder firmly, then jumped— disappearing into the night with the scattering cargo. Oscar and Clive followed soon after.

Asya lingered.

She looked down through the opening at the people below—scattered figures racing across the surface, scooping up parts raining from above.

And then she saw her.

A fiery red head turned upward, watching in awe. Mae.

For a heartbeat, the child thought she saw someone familiar. Then a bronze-and-black cybernetic leg dropped at her feet.

She gasped, bent her rusted leg just enough to pick it up, and stared skyward.

The ship had already passed.

Asya had made it out of the ship without incident.

She'd closed the hatch and resealed the emptied crates—something she hadn't told the others. She escaped through another maintenance hatch, slipping away undetected, leaving the sky people to open crates filled with nothing when they reached their port above the clouds.

Below, the plan had come together better than anyone hoped.

Not only had their bees brought in the pollen, but others—not originally involved—began trickling into the shop, offering salvaged pieces.

Not every item was undamaged, of course. But that only helped conceal what they'd done.

Together, they had delivered something far greater than stolen tech.

They had delivered change.

And in doing so, they had ignited something new—something powerful—in the hearts of the next generation.

Broken Hearted Plead

The day was hot and humid, the clouds nearly non-existent in the sky. Lydia had been working on house chores while the kids played on the Nintendo Switch in the living room, and the teenager sat in her room drawing on her digital tablet.

It was no different than any other spring day—except maybe summer was poking its head out sooner than anyone really wanted.

Lydia's husband had taken it upon himself to go to a nearby park to work out. It was something he felt good doing. See, her husband worked from home five days a week and hardly ever left the house. Running the three blocks to the park was his way of escaping the confining walls of a home-turned-office-building.

Lydia knew so much had been weighing on her husband's shoulders for some time. He hadn't taken to working from home well.

Jared was a sort of social butterfly, although he would deny it if you asked him. He needed to be around his peers to collaborate on projects. Often enough, Jared would rant to Lydia about how he would wait for hours upon hours for a response on the team's app—when it would've only taken a few steps from one desk to another to get what he needed.

Lydia knew he was quite troubled with his working situation, but he had no choice in the matter—being a contracting software engineer.

It was mid-April, and Lydia was in her bedroom folding laundry while watching one of her shows when she heard slamming doors and loud banging sounds.

"What is that?" Often, she spoke to herself when something odd was happening in the house and she was alone.

Dropping the shirt she was folding back into the white basket at her feet, she left the bedroom and descended the stairs—only to meet the flushed, sweaty face of her husband, Jared.

"What were all those sounds? What is happening?"

Trying to go around him, she moved toward the basement door. But Jared shifted past her. That's when she saw the damage: a hole in the wall nearest to the basement, where his office was.

Feeling the heat of her anger rise to her face, she swallowed it down slowly.

"Jared, what is the matter? What happened?"

Looking her dead in the eyes, his voice held such rage. "You don't want me to talk to you right now."

With that, Jared grabbed his wallet from the basket on the entryway table and ripped his keys from the hooks above.

Lydia watched as he pushed his way out of the house and got into the sedan. The tires peeled out of the driveway—

rage in motion.

The younger two children had retreated to their older sister's room during the chaos. When they came downstairs, they asked, "What happened? Where did Dad go?"

Lydia felt a knot form in her stomach. She didn't know how to answer. "I'm not sure. Daddy's just angry, and I don't know why. Let's not worry about it. Go ahead and play your games."

Watching her children return to the couch, she descended into the basement where Jared's office had been set up in a non-conforming bedroom.

A cup of coffee had been thrown across the room, splattering brown liquid on the wall. Jared had completely cleared his desk by hand—ripping off his monitors and flipping the standing desk.

Swallowing the knot rising in her throat, she couldn't bring herself to clean up his mess. She always cleaned up after his rage fits.

Not this time.

Lydia returned to the main floor. "Don't go into the basement. It's a mess."

She retreated to the bedroom to finish what she was doing. It was five in the afternoon.

Time for dinner.

Lydia tried to keep to their normal routine, unaware the entire night would spiral into chaos.

*H*ours passed. Lydia spent the evening preparing the kids for bed and going through their tuck-in routine.

It was already after nine o'clock. Jared still hadn't

returned. Worry began to set in.

Holding the phone to her ear, she listened to it ring and ring until it hit voicemail. "Jared, where are you? I have surgery in the morning, remember?"

Voicemail. He was clearly ignoring her calls, and she didn't understand why.

Taking a deep breath, she shut everything down in the house and tried to distract herself by binge-watching her current Netflix show.

Glancing down at her phone, she saw it was nearly 10:30 p.m. She called her mother, who lived nearly an hour away in the city where Lydia was scheduled to have her gallbladder removed.

"No, I don't know where he is or what he's doing. He took the car, and I don't know if he's coming home. Would you be willing to pick me up and take me to surgery?"

Her mother calmly agreed.

"I'll let you know if anything changes, and if I truly need you to come get me or not."

What Lydia didn't know was that this night marked the beginning of a terrible road in her marriage. Nearly ten years of shared life was circling the drain—for reasons completely unknown to her.

Jared did return—but completely drunk, almost unrecognizable.

"Jared, you need to sleep. I need to sleep. You're supposed to take me in for my surgery."

Fighting him to get ready for bed was the hardest part.

She thought he was asleep. That was foolish.

When Jared had arrived home, he'd thrown his wallet across the street and his car keys down the road. Thankfully, they had installed security cameras the summer before. Lydia was able to use the recordings to trace where he'd tossed everything.

Glancing over at what she thought was her passed-out husband, Lydia slipped out of the bedroom and left the house to search for his belongings.

Cold droplets began to fall from the sky.

She looked up. It didn't matter.

The smell of rain grounded her in the middle of the day's chaos—bringing her back to what meant everything. She had taken a vow to stand by her husband, through the worst and the best.

Crossing the street, she found his wallet and tucked it into her pocket.

"Oh, Jared." Her words were soft—meant only for herself.

Crossing back, she scoured the sidewalk and the grass, aiming her phone's flashlight in the direction the keys had been thrown.

Suddenly, Jared ran past her. The sounds he made weren't just those of a drunk—they were wild, erratic. Intoxicated beyond reason.

"Jared!" She tried not to shout too loudly—it was after one in the morning. "Jared, please! You need to go back inside and sleep. I'm trying to find your keys."

He ran down the street to where his keys lay on the asphalt, picked them up, and handed them over without a word.

After a short struggle, Lydia got her husband back inside and into bed.

What she didn't know was that this was only the tip of the iceberg. Jared was slipping into a midlife crisis—one she wouldn't piece together fully until a year and a half later.

Chaos took over the lives of Lydia and Jared—mostly Jared, who was living in a secret identity crisis while leading Lydia to believe he only had certain issues that needed solving.

Battling suicidal ideations, Jared became Lydia's full priority. She often put off large extended family gatherings. More and more, she ignored her children to focus all her energy on her husband—afraid he might teeter off the edge and make good on the plans he so easily shared with her.

Living in a constant state of fear and sadness, Lydia watched as the closeness they once had faded into a black void of nothingness.

Slowly, Jared began to take on some of the spirituality Lydia practiced, showing interest in the fun festival she went to twice a year where mystic shops came together and psychics gave readings at low prices. He had begun to see one of the readers who practiced Norse rune reading. He actually took the readings to heart, as they seemed to come true for him in eerie ways.

"Jared, I know that you've been holding back some truth of what happened."

Lydia stood near the door of his office, watching him work at his computer. One earbud dangled from his headphones so he could hear her.

"I swear to you, I am not out messing around on you. I don't have time for myself, let alone to go looking for another woman."

She tried to ignore the feeling in her gut—the one everyone calls intuition.

It was always the same conversation, over and over. Every time it ended with Lydia in silence, leaving Jared to his business and herself to the bedroom to cry.

Things had gotten so bad between them because Jared had stopped showing her affection. And when Lydia pointed it out, he'd flirt with her here and there—a butt pinch or a boob grab—as if that could smooth everything over for a little while.

One day, Lydia heard the garage door and footsteps—Jared leaving with the kids in tow. They were excited about some new RC toys he had bought them on a spur-of-the-moment shopping trip.

Wandering down from the bedroom, she made her way into his office and found his computer unlocked—something that was very unlike him.

Taking the opportunity, she began snooping through the messages on the chat application he often used for gaming and networking.

She searched keywords: "wife," "leave."

And what she found broke her.

So many disheartening things he had said about her. About their marriage. About his desire to leave. All from that year.

The ball of pain and nausea grew in the pit of her

stomach. Her worst fear—her intuition—had been right. He had been unfaithful, at least emotionally. Maybe more.

She felt like she was going to vomit.

Getting up from his desk, she ran to the bathroom and emptied her stomach into the toilet. Clutching the seat, she felt the heat of tears spilling down her cheeks.

"I knew it. I knew it!"

Wiping her mouth with toilet paper, she hung her head low and flushed.

Deep, guttural sobs erupted from her chest. Hot streams of grief poured from her eyes. It all hurt so badly. All the effort she had put into keeping their marriage together—how could he say those things and still come to bed every night? Still play with her hair, kiss her goodnight?

Standing from the floor, Lydia wiped her face. The knot in her stomach had become a heavy, throbbing weight in her chest. Her body shook with the shock of the truth finally coming out.

She had begged and begged for honesty to return to their marriage. But not like this. Not through hidden messages on an unlocked screen. Not because he forgot to protect the secret.

Her world was spinning. Lydia felt like she was going crazy.

Every fear she'd ever had about being in a relationship again—after all those years of marriage—they were happening.

C limbing out of the basement, Lydia found herself sitting in her bedroom, across from her altar.

She was a practicing pagan. She gave offerings to many gods and goddesses.

Staring at the table that held all her sacred tools, she felt the urge to cry again.

Dragging her fingers over her eyes, she broke down, bawling in front of the gods she called upon every day.

"Oh, what did I do to deserve this?"

Wiping her face, she moved into the private bathroom to blow away the snot and grief building up.

"He told me it wasn't me. That it was all him. How could he lie to me—and say all those cruel things?"

Staring at herself in the mirror, she met her own green eyes.

"What did you do?"

She saw her own anger staring back. Turning away, she drew in the deepest breath she could manage before heading to confront her husband.

Lydia had never been one to let things lie.

She had to face them.

She had to face him.

The priority now was identifying the woman he'd been speaking of—the one he said made him feel "drunk." The one who made him burn his vows to ash.

I n the garage, Jared sat watching the kids play with their new RC cars in the driveway.

Lydia crept up behind him and leaned near his head.

She whispered, "So who was the woman who made you drunk—who made you realize how much of a mistake your marriage was?" Every word was soaked in venom. Her whole body vibrated with rage.

Jared paused his mobile game and turned to meet her eyes. "Not here. Let's go inside to talk."

That evening, their teenager cared for the younger siblings while Jared and Lydia sat in the basement and talked about everything she had found.

Jared argued that what he'd said in those messages was true , but that it no longer was. Everything he said came with a caveat—an excuse about the headspace he'd been in, the crisis he'd been going through.

Lydia argued that she would never say such things about him. That she would never have done anything like that.

Leaving Jared on the couch, she walked to the storage room off the sitting room and retrieved a suitcase. "Jared, I've been contemplating leaving you for quite some time. I've tried, and tried, to give you time. To heal. To be with me."

Turning with the suitcase in hand, she made her way to the stairs. "I'm going to go stay with my friend for a few days—or until I feel like I want to come back."

Jared watched her go, unable to move. He sat frozen on the couch, trying to fight the overwhelming urge to hurl his phone at the wall.

ydia left.

Now Jared was in charge—of the children, of the home, of everything. He tried, over and over, to text her. Even called her, though he hated talking on the phone.

But Lydia never answered.

It devastated him. That she had actually left. That she had the strength to walk away.

Depression pressed heavily on his shoulders. Panic attacks came more often—ones that only used to subside with Lydia's touch.

Functioning without her was becoming harder. The kids had questions.

Where's Mommy?

Why did she leave?

He told them lies.

He couldn't bring himself to say that he had broken their mother's heart. That he had caused all the tears, all the lonely nights.

He used to tell Lydia how much he appreciated what she did for the house. Now, more than ever.

Sleep was impossible without her next to him.

When he saw her online in that same chat application—playing games—he had to resist the urge to ask if she wanted to play with him.

How could he have screwed up nearly thirteen years of marriage? Desperation started to set in.

One afternoon, Jared left the children with their near-adult sister and went to the local mystic store in search of some kind of guidance. This wasn't something he usually did. No—this was more Lydia's wheelhouse.

His wife had made more of an impact on him than he'd ever admitted. And now, he was looking for help from a god or an entity of some kind.

Stepping into the store, thick with the scent of incense and burning candles, Jared was greeted by a smiling woman.

"Hello! Welcome to New Awakenings. Is there anything I can help you with?"

Jared—being the straight-to-the-point type—quickly got to his question. "Yes. Um…" A pause. He searched for the right way to say it. "I'm looking for a way—or something—that can help with turning back time. Or maybe a god that… dabbles with time?"

The woman's brow lifted slightly. She turned and began walking toward a shelf lined with statues, polished glass reflecting their bronze and silver finishes. "Well, there's the god Kronos."

Jared knew what he was getting himself into. He hadn't truly believed before. But now, he was desperate enough to give whatever he had if it would bring his wife back.

"Please. Show me."

The sales associate guided him to a bronze statue of the god and then walked him to the bookshelves. She pulled several volumes down. "These would be helpful in what you're looking for. There's a lot of good information on Kronos."

Jared followed her through the store, arms slowly filling with books, incense, candles—everything he needed to build an altar. Price didn't matter. All that mattered was results.

Leaving the shop with two black bags, Jared stood beside his truck, key fob in hand, frozen. He was lost in thought. Realizing he was holding his breath, he gasped for air.

Climbing into the truck, he fought off a panic attack

long enough to drive home and set up his new altar to the god of time.

Two days passed since Jared's out-of-character purchase, and the weekend finally came.

The younger two kids had gone with their grandmother. The teenager was out with friends.

Alone, Jared sat in front of the altar to Kronos. He lit incense and kneeled. "Kronos, god of time, I beckon thee. I am desperate. I've messed up something very precious to me—something I thought didn't matter... but it did."

The weight in his chest deepened. He fell silent.

Then, sitting up, he lit a black candle beside the statue and continued. "I lost the one person who made my world stop spinning out of control. The one person who grounded me when I floated too high."

Following the steps he'd read in one of his new books, Jared bathed himself and the statue in incense smoke.

Now cleansed, he continued to pour all his wants and needs into the universe—praying to Kronos. Pleading for his wife to return his calls. For her to come home.

Forgiveness was all he wanted. To be understood—for the crisis he had gone through. He admitted to himself that he had said cruel things. He had even said their vows meant nothing to him. His head sank into his hands. His whispered prayers continued.

A wave of spinning overtook him. The dizziness was almost too much. He stood up, let the candles burn themselves out to complete the spellwork, and left the room to retire for the evening.

That night, Jared's dreams were filled with visions of him fighting for Lydia.

In every version of the dream, he failed.

Filthy rich? She still walked away.

Charming? Begging? Weeping?

She left anyway.

He woke with his heart aching, clutching his chest.

Sitting up in bed, he looked into the dark room—and froze.

There was a figure at the end of the bed.

Blinking a few times, thinking it might be his imagination, he watched as the dark figure moved... around the bed... to Lydia's side.

His legs felt impossibly heavy, as though weighed down by gravity itself.

Fear sat like copper on the back of his tongue as the figure glided around the room—taking in every little detail of the woman who had once been there.

A sound emerged from the blackness. Soft at first. Then louder, and louder, until it filled Jared's entire body.

Screaming, Jared sat up to find sunlight creeping through the curtains.

He gripped the blankets, then threw them off. Heart pounding. Scanning the room, he stood. Something was... off.

The bedroom looked different. The walls were no longer the same warm neutral—now a bluish gray, accented in black. Turning slowly, Jared realized the décor had shifted completely. The new colors. The details. It was all Lydia's style.

Then he saw the dresser. Not in its usual place. And not in its usual form. Painted black and purple. Different handles. On top, photos. Photos of him. Photos of the children. Their wedding photo—laughing, smearing cake in each other's faces. Opening drawers, he found trinkets. Jewelry. Familiar pieces.

But no clothes of his.

Only the bottom drawer held anything that belonged to him—and even then, just boxes of what looked like memory items. His stomach twisted. Panic rose.

Slamming the drawer shut, rocking the framed photos, he rushed to the bathroom. Opening the drawer where they had always kept their medication, he found only Lydia's things. Cold medicine. A bottle of lotion.

No sign of him.

He turned and pushed open the closet. Near empty—except for Lydia's new shelving. "What is this? What is happening?"

He ran through the house.

Each child's room had changed—different paint, different layouts.

He flew down the stairs, breath ragged. His head spinning. "So much changed... and so little of is here."

And then he saw it.

A folded program lying in a stack of papers on the kitchen counter. Two years old. The date at the top: 2024.

The truth hit like a freight train. "But I failed..."

Picking up the program, he began to read.

The eulogy was written by Lydia. Every sentence soaked in her voice. "This can't be... I don't understand."

Tears burned hot behind his eyes.

And then, again: ticking. Faint, but growing louder. Coming from the basement.

His eyes shifted to the basement door—still bearing the metal gaming signs Lydia had placed there when they'd first bought the house.

He stared at the signs. The ticking grew louder.

Hand trembling, Jared reached for the doorknob, pulled it open, and stepped down into the dark.

Turning to reach for the light switch, he descended the stairs to what he thought was the basement, when Jared suddenly found himself walking down the staircase from the upper level of the house again.

Blinking, he looked at the banister—it wasn't the same one that led to the basement. "What the hell?"

Standing at the top of the stairs behind him was the large, dark figure—watching silently as Jared continued his path toward the first floor. The farther down he went, the ticking faded. Now, he heard crying. It came from the basement.

Again, Jared stood at the door, his hand hovering over the knob. Hesitating.

Finally, he pulled together the courage to open it. He stepped onto the actual stairs that led into the basement. Curving around the corner, he recognized the sound—Lydia crying. And then the sound of her vomiting in the bathroom.

"Oh..."

He moved closer. Lydia emerged from the bathroom, her face wracked with pain. She didn't see him. She walked right past.

Jared stood frozen, then turned toward his office—remembering he had left his computer open. "Lydia read everything…"

His skin began to tingle. His breath caught in his lungs again.

It his fault. Especially because this time, the screen had been left on one message in particular. Words he had once confided to someone, thinking it was safe:

"After the first year, I knew that I didn't want to be married. I just stayed, because I knew it would destroy her."

Sitting down in his computer chair, he felt the full weight of what he had done. How much that sentence sounded like something Lydia's would've said. How cruel. How similar. How deep that wound must have cut.

Closing his eyes, a single tear crested his lower eyelid.

When he opened them again, he was no longer in his office chair. He sat on the old couch in the living room of the house Lydia had lived in before they started dating.

Sitting up straight, he slapped his hands against the cushions—startled. It looked exactly like the night they'd met. The night they laughed. The night they drank too much. The night he felt like he had known Lydia forever.

Turning, Jared saw the black-shrouded figure sitting on the far side of the L-shaped couch. His heart rate spiked.

He stood, shouting, "What are you? Who are you?"

Dry-swallowing, he rushed toward the shadow figure—but stumbled.

Suddenly, he was sitting at a table at their wedding. Sweat poured from his forehead. His eyes darted across the room—from family member to family member.

Silence fell. Then, music.

He turned to see Lydia, arm in arm with her father, walking toward the stage. She smiled. Jared's breath hitched—he felt the butterflies all over again.

Then he blinked—and was beside her as she gave birth to their first child. He looked down. Blue scrubs. A surgical hat. The nurse passed by holding their baby, calling him over to cut the cord.

Jared stood—only to find himself in yet another version of their life. This time, back at the house. Alone.

The décor looked the same. But pieces were missing. Lydia's things. The children's things. Room by room, he searched.

"Future, past... what could be? What would have been?"

A deep gasp burst from his chest—he hadn't even realized he'd stopped breathing.

Sliding down the wall of the hallway near the front door, he propped his feet against the opposite wall, pulling his hair from his face. Resting his head on his knees, he tried to steady his breath.

Time. It all came back to time.

Standing up, Jared stared up and yelled as loudly as he could. "Kronos! I know this is you!"

A cold, dark rush of black water enveloped his body, pulling him through the floor of the hall, smothering him from head to toe. The darkness was like nothing Jared had ever experienced before—it was more like an empty space void of life itself. The sound of ticking filled his ears, the sound associated with most grandfather clocks.

Landing with a sudden thud on a hard surface, the sound of large bell tower bells rang out. Blinking furiously, Jared's eyesight came back in a blur. Slowly clearing up, Jared found himself standing in a large field of grain. Pieces of the grain were falling from the stalks, creating the ticking sound he was hearing. The eerie sound made his skin crawl as he watched every little piece fall, creating the sound in a much more rhythmic way.

His ears started to ring with the ticking, much like tinnitus. Grabbing at his ears, he spun around, realizing he was completely surrounded by the grain.

SWOOP! A gust of wind pushed the hair over the back of his neck. A moment passed, and it happened again. *SWOOP!*

Jared started to run through the large, endless field of ticking grain. A large, swirling shadow passed over him. Looking up, he just missed the gleaming light off what seemed to be a blade of some sort. Coming down, it sliced through the grain with little effort. The heads of the grain slammed into the ground, giving the sound of bells hitting against one another. The ticking seemed to become much more intense.

The beat of Jared's heart grew harder, harsher, as he ran, as if he was trying to find the finish line in a marathon. Row after row of grain stalks smacked him in the face, until he heard the deep laugh come from all around him, stopping him in his tracks.

Suddenly, everything came to a deafening silence, and all of the shadow cast by the stalks of grain slithered together into one single mass in front of Jared. Slowly, the mass of shadow grew larger and larger, taking on the shape of a man—long black flowing robes with one hand extended outward holding a scythe. The figure stood nearly eight feet tall, and there were no discernible features.

Jared heard his heart pounding in his ears, and his mouth instantaneously felt dry. Was this the grim reaper? Was this death?

It was at that moment Jared realized not only was it silent, but everything around him had ceased. Time had frozen all around him.

"Time you waste, throw it away. You run away and hide from all the chances it gives you."

The voice was a deep bass that vibrated the soul, giving rise to goose pimples all over the flesh.

"You beg and plead for the most precious thing to you, although you yourself don't understand what it is you're asking for."

Jared stood before this massive figure. His knees felt weak, as if he had just run a ten-mile marathon. Taking everything he had to keep himself from collapsing to the ground, he was confused about what the figure spoke about.

Jared knew exactly what he had prayed for—who he pleaded for. Eyes widening, it now dawned on the man who or what stood before him. What powerful being rattled him to his core.

"Kronos?"

His words were much quieter than he had expected when he spoke out. Was it fear?

The figure seemed to grow larger before him. The very presence of the god was overwhelming and intimidating.

"I want Lydia to return to me. I want her forgiveness, her love. She is the only person who brings me peace, who brings me comfort."

The large shadow figure boomed with a deep, boisterous laughter, both hands grasping onto the scythe planted into the soil as if to hold himself more upright. The god laughed for a good while, making the man before him question everything that had just poured from his lips.

Silence overwhelmed Jared suddenly as Kronos leaned over him, still using the scythe like a walking stick.

"You beg for someone you pushed away. You plead for someone whose heart you separated from your own?"

Walking around the mortal before him, Kronos seemed to take in the flesh of the man inch by inch. Peering deeply into the soul of the man, he stopped, pondering if it was worth his time.

"I have shown you what it would have been like if you were successful that night. I have shown you what it was like for her to find out your secrets and the pain she suffered alone. I have shown you some of the best days of both your lives—days she regrets because she now lives in pain, wanting you. Wanting a man who would let go of everything for selfish reasons. For a man who would betray her behind her back emotionally and not have the decency to be honest about it all.

"Yet, here you are before me pleading for her to be back at your side? For what? Will she have to do everything for you on your time? Wait for you? Make all the decisions? Wait for you to be okay again to touch her, to love her?"

The laughter boomed from the dark figure once more. "You know nothing of what you desire, what you plead for."

Turning, the large robed figure of Kronos melted away,

splashing into the earth like water, leaving behind the scythe standing in the earth. The large blade started to hover towards the heads of the grain. Time started again as the ticking of the falling grains came sudden and loud. The scythe skimmed over Jared's head, suddenly taking some of the grain. The fall of the stalks rocked together like loud church bells.

Jared's legs collapsed under him as the scythe had flown over. The weakness overtook his body. Feeling the sudden flare of sweat on his forehead, his head began to swim.

It felt like hours, days, maybe weeks?

Jared stood in the realm between time, his head lost with the rhythm of the ticking grain. Every now and again he would catch a glimpse of Kronos—or so he thought was the god. He was alone. Alone with his thoughts. Thoughts that bounced from A to Z.

His mind drove him insane. He couldn't sleep. He couldn't get it to shut down. When he was home, he had medicine. He had Lydia. He could focus on his programs and games.

Now he was alone, in a space plagued by a repetitive sound and his thoughts.

"You know nothing of what you desire, what you plead for."

Over and over, he contemplated the last thing Kronos said to him before leaving him in this place. Leaving him to go insane.

Pacing back and forth through the spaces left open by the scythe, Jared tapped the temples of his head with both hands rapidly.

"What did he mean by that?"

Obliviousness was a trait of Jared's, and it wasn't always cut and dry for the man. Jared didn't always see what was in front of him, and often that was how he lost things that were precious to him. Like time. Love. People.

Whenever Jared would attempt to sleep in the field of time, Kronos would send him through new scenarios of "what ifs" with and without his wife and family. He lived out his nightmares and things he had told his wife out of anger.

It was pure madness—everything he was experiencing just to learn an important lesson.

It was a weekend when Lydia finally returned. The house was quiet—eerily quiet—as she stepped through the front door. The children were gone, and Jared's truck sat in the driveway. A large weight settled in her chest.

Her teenager had texted her earlier to let her know she'd be out with friends. Lydia had kept in close contact with her since leaving to take a break. The understanding and support from her eldest had been unexpectedly comforting, especially since nothing could be hidden from her.

Lydia headed straight for the basement, assuming Jared would be there. At his office door, she paused. He wasn't at his desk. "Odd," she murmured, checking her watch. It was nearly two in the afternoon. He should have been awake by now.

She glanced at the altar to Kronos, lingering for only a moment before moving on. She checked the kitchen—no sign he'd made coffee. Ascending the stairs to the bedroom, Lydia hesitated again, the weight in her chest pressing heavier.

What she was about to do would hurt. But she had already done so much grieving. It had to get better, right?

She turned the knob and slowly opened the door. The room was dim. Sunlight filtered through the top of the blackout curtains, outlining Jared's body on the bed. At first glance, he appeared to be asleep.

Lydia sat gently on the edge of the bed. She watched him for a long moment. Then she reached out and shook his shoulder.

"Jared?" No response.

She shook him harder. "Jared, it's time to wake up. Jared!"

Climbing partially onto the bed in alarm, Lydia checked his pulse. It was there. Normal. She pulled down the blanket and rubbed her knuckles into his sternum—hard. Still nothing.

Pulling out her phone, she called for emergency help. "Yes, I need some help at my house. My husband won't wake up. He's breathing, his pulse is fine... I've shaken him and rubbed his sternum without any luck."

She stayed calm—more than she expected of herself—though a storm of panic roiled in her gut. Could this be another attempt to take his own life? Or something else?

Lydia met the paramedics at the door and led them upstairs. Minutes later, she was following the ambulance to the hospital.

Hours passed. Jared had been admitted. Every test came back empty. No answers. He was in a coma—one no one could explain.

Lydia sat beside him, her hand wrapped around his. She watched his still body, silently begging for any response. His mother sobbed in the arms of her partner on the other side of the bed. The children remained with their other grandmother.

Evening came. The room emptied, and Lydia found herself alone with Jared.

Her eyes burned from tears. She leaned down and kissed his cheek, whispering into his ear:

"Now you can finally have the alone time you've always wanted."

Choking down a sob, Lydia grabbed her purse from the chair and fled the room.

Hunter's Moon

ears had passed since that fateful day that brought Revna to the Bone Collectors—a child of ten who had performed an act never expected of someone her age. Now, at twenty, she had grown into a woman with a high reputation as one of the best trackers the guild had.

Standing high above the camp in one of the outlook towers, the land below looked almost peaceful to her, as if there weren't feral beasts stalking through the shadows. The thought of people being unable to travel the roads from town to town without the risk of their children being ripped away made her sick to her stomach—nearly made her head spin with the memory of her first bloodletting. Losing both of her parents in such a way had ripped something deep inside her open, pouring out feelings of revenge and anger she hadn't understood until she became an adult.

Leaning against the stained wood railing, her long black hair dangled over the near twenty-foot drop, her gray eyes following the party nearing the gates of the encampment. She recognized the men below—two carrying a deer between them, while two others dragged a man in chains of silver.

The silver ring of a horn touched her lips as she filled it with air, pushing the loud sound into the sky above. "Doland's party has returned!"

Pulling the horn to her mouth once more, she sounded the alarm again, then hung it on the post near the ladder that led down to the base. Wasting no time, Revna climbed down, skipping the last three rungs and dropping with a thud onto her feet. The leather of her boots was well-worn, creased in the proper places, showing how much running and jumping they'd seen.

Other guild members moved in to open the gate and let the men in. Three took the deer off the shoulders of the overburdened pair. Moving through the crowd, Revna watched the men part like water as she approached the prisoner. His head hung low to his chest, his hands dangling as the others held him up under the arms.

"How did you get so lucky catching this one?" she asked, turning her gaze to the leader of the party, a man at least two feet taller than her who cradled his left arm across his chest.

She noticed the injury and, with it, realized they hadn't made it back with all their members.

"If it weren't for Leo and Otis's quick work, the rest of us wouldn't be here," he said.

Revna looked around, noting the two names weren't among them.

"Head to the infirmary and have your arm looked at," she ordered. "I'll help escort this beastman to the holding cells."

Turning from her fellow guild member, Revna motioned for the men to allow a fresh pair of hands to take the prisoner.

Taking the lead, she often looked back as they walked toward the holding cells. The smell of the silver chains burning into the man's flesh was putrid. The pain they caused was unimaginable to her. Not that Revna much cared for the beasts they captured—for the order, what was done to them afterward was, in her mind, for the good of the human populace.

The thought of what this one had likely been doing before her fellow hunters tracked him and his pack made her angry. The sickness she felt from memories locked away crept into her gut.

Reaching the large, heavy-gated holding area, Revna banged on it with the pommel of the short sword secured at her left hip. "Hey!"

Her voice carried through the bars to the guards on duty. One of them—a man about six feet tall, dressed in brown hunting leathers—approached the gate. The distinct jingle of keys at his hip was easy to track.

"Could you move like you have a mission? We have a new prisoner!"

The man knew exactly who was yelling. Although she could be intimidating, some in the guild still didn't believe a woman belonged.

The men holding the prisoner were getting antsy as the beast began to regain consciousness. Even restrained in silver, some retained strength through the pain. The sound of the lock disengaging brought a wave of relief. Revna turned with a scowl.

"Sure, take your time. Help them secure the prisoner fast—he's starting to wake. Hate to see another man torn apart."

The man frowned as he passed her and relieved some of the weight from the other two, escorting them through the gate toward the specially made cells of iron and silver meant to hold werebeasts.

Revna remained behind, standing at the gate. Relief washed over her knowing the prisoner had made it inside. Her hands gripped the heavy metal door as she pushed it closed behind the men.

Leaning against the gate, Revna was suddenly startled by a scream.

"Must be the new prisoner."

Deep inside the holding cells, instruments of torture awaited creatures like him—beds of silver needles that pressed slowly into their flesh until they broke or were taken by high-ranking officers for experimentation.

After growing up among the Bone Collectors, and with help from a small village just outside the main camp, Revna had learned from Reinfield that the guild's ultimate goal was to find a "cure" for the afflicted. She believed deeply in their mission—perhaps more so than some of the other members, or so she thought.

Revna often forgot, in the heat of her own need for revenge, that every Bone Collector had their own reasons for joining. Though they didn't often share them, many believed in the cause just as fiercely as she did.

Hearing the two men she had initially come to the cells

with chuckling as they made their way back to the gate, Revna lifted herself from the warmed metal to allow them through.

"Prisoner secured!" one of them called, sarcasm lacing his voice. He added a mock salute that earned only a blank stare from her. Men like that had long ago learned they wouldn't get a rise out of her; Revna had decided years before it was better not to give them the satisfaction.

Giving a slight nod, she turned on her heel and walked away without a word. Her left hand curled tightly around the leather-wrapped pommel of her sword, knuckles turning white from the pressure.

Take a deep breath, don't let them get to you, she reminded herself. Sucking in a full breath, she let it slowly escape through parted lips as she neared the outer gate, counting steadily in her head. With each breath, her shoulders loosened.

"Revna!"

She stopped short of the stained wooden gate, eyes closed a moment before turning toward the familiar voice.

"Oh. Reinfield! How have you been?"

The older gentleman who had saved her all those years ago, now with hair turning silver, smiled. "I am well. The council would like you to return tomorrow mid-morning for a meeting."

That usually meant a new mission—welcome news if it meant fewer hours surrounded by guild members who still didn't believe she belonged.

"Alright. I'll meet you and the other council members mid-morning."

Reinfield nodded and took his leave. Revna lingered a

moment longer at the gate, watching him disappear into the shadows beyond. Two guards coming on for the evening shift approached the wall path.

"Better head out! We're about to lock down."

The guards moved to the thick, crudely forged iron poles driven several feet into the ground. These anchored the heavy ropes that controlled the massive gate doors—weighted with rock to close quickly in an emergency.

Revna took her cue and passed through to the other side just as the doors creaked shut behind her. The weight of the gate made the walls shudder, small splinters of wood fluttering through the air.

Though the encampment gave the illusion of safety, Revna had always found greater peace among the villagers of Eyvindara. Reinfield and the council had agreed it was better for her to live among them than in a camp full of men often caught in the euphoria of returning from a successful hunt. Some forgot their manners, and more than a few ended up with black eyes when they tested her patience.

When she came of age, Reinfield had arranged for a village household to take her in until she could live independently. The villagers had accepted the young Bone Collector, even if some were initially surprised a woman belonged to the guild. Reinfield had told only the necessary leaders about her past, securing her place. From that day forward, Revna devoted herself not just to the Bone Collectors, but to the people of Eyvindara as well.

She took a slow breath and closed her eyes, letting her shoulders fall. The first step down the path toward home felt like a reset. As she walked, she continued to count her breaths. The more steps she took, the less tension she carried.

Revna knew the trail home like the back of her hand and could walk it blindfolded. When she opened her eyes again, the village was closer. One of the men approached from the opposite direction, a ring of rabbits swinging at his side.

"Looks like you had a good catch today!"

He turned at the sound of her voice, his scowl softening into a smile. "Oh! Yes, all my rabbit traps worked this time. Thanks for the advice, Revna."

She smiled, falling into step beside him. "You're welcome. Let me know if you want more help with your hunting."

The glow of torches lit the trees as they neared the village. The man broke off toward the square, where his family waited. Revna turned toward her modest hut—her home.

The villagers knew her well by now, and most respected her. She often spent time helping with small tasks and had a special bond with the elders, who had once given their time to care for an orphan girl. That care had shaped her fiercely protective instincts.

Most nights, even after the village had gone quiet, Revna would patrol the perimeter—scouting for the same monsters that had taken her parents.

The next morning arrived without incident. Running on her usual six hours of sleep, Revna was up and moving through her daily routine. In the woods, she reset rabbit traps and studied new markings on the trees. She constantly re-memorized the area around the village and the camp.

Every sign—whether man-made or animal—was noted. Some called her paranoid, but those who knew her role as a tracker understood her precision.

She straightened suddenly at the sound of voices. Her gray eyes found several village men heading out to hunt, bows slung over their shoulders. She relaxed.

Checking the final trap line, she started toward the Bone Collectors' camp, knowing she'd arrive earlier than requested. That usually meant there would be work to do.

Closer to camp, Revna noticed ruts in the path. Kneeling, she touched the dirt lightly. Her fingers, trained by years of tracking, told her what had made them and how quickly it had moved.

The grooves were deep. Whatever it was, it had been heavy—and likely important.

She broke into a jog.

As she neared the camp, her suspicions were confirmed. A covered wagon made of wood and iron stood just inside the gate. The horses were being led away for food and water.

"Oy! What's got you in a hurry?!"

Shielding her eyes from the sunrise, she looked up to find Doland in the tower above the gate. She didn't answer.

Her attention returned to the wagon. A symbol— crossed bones—was branded into the wood. It clearly belonged to the guild.

But who had brought it here, and what was inside?

It had come from another Bone Collector camp. That much was clear. But the rest? Revna intended to find out.

Passing through the gate, Revna's ears were hit with a

wave of noise that had been shielded by the walls around the camp. Her eyes took in the vast number of guild members spread across the training yard. Many were dressed in traditional hunting gear, each marked with the crossed bones emblem. Some faces were unfamiliar, others she recognized—men laughing and sharing stories of close encounters with beasts beyond the borders.

Not paying much attention as she walked, Revna nearly collided with two men carrying a hefty boar toward the fire pits.

"Hey! Watch where you're walking!" one of them barked.

She stopped abruptly, narrowly avoiding the carcass, and watched as the men passed, shaking their heads. Pinching her eyes into a glare, she continued toward the large longhouse where the council often held meetings and welcomed guests.

The building, fashioned from the wood of trees that once stood on the very land they now walked, had been smoothed and sealed to what Renfield called "perfection." Ornate carvings of hunters and beasts adorned the structure, and the front featured a long wooden deck where elders could sit or address the men when necessary.

As Revna moved through the busy camp, dodging men hurrying to and from chores or preparing for missions, she spotted Renfield speaking with another man who had striking white hair. She kept her distance, watching as they spoke for a few minutes before shaking hands and disappearing into the longhouse.

Glancing at the shadows on the ground, she judged it

was nearly time for her to enter. She shook out her hands at her sides, flexing her fingers. *I sure hope I get to take a mission alone. I need some time away from these jokesters.*

Silencing her thoughts and slowing her breathing, Revna approached the longhouse door.

What exactly was she waiting for?

Before she could open it, the door swung wide from within. A wall of warmth and sound hit her immediately—too many bodies in too tight a space. The man who had opened the door gestured her inside, stepping aside to let her pass.

Taking her cue, Revna entered the longhouse, nodding her thanks. As she walked deeper into the crowded space, she spotted familiar and unfamiliar Bone Collector faces alike. She wasn't used to receiving assignments in front of an audience, and though she wasn't the nervous type, the situation was unexpected.

Nodding brief hellos and acknowledgments, she made her way to Renfield, the one person she always felt had her back. She took a position of attention beside him just as he turned, smiling faintly as her boots clicked together.

"Oh! Yes, here she is now," he said.

He motioned the man in front of him toward Revna. The man, dressed in black-dyed leathers, had piercing blue eyes and a presence that could freeze a room. He appeared to be near her age and stood a full foot taller than Renfield— who she already had two inches on herself.

The man extended his left hand.

Revna looked at it a moment, then reached out and met his grip with firm pressure, her knuckles nearly turning white.

"Revna," Renfield said, his eyes lingering on her with a slight smile. "I'd like you to meet Ozias. He's come with a group of volunteers from another Bone Collector camp. He's one of their top hunters."

Revna nodded as they shook hands, masking her lack of interest with a polite tone only Renfield and a few other elder council members could recognize.

"Ozias, it is truly an honor to meet you," she said smoothly. "Are all these men joining our ranks for the time being, or is this a permanent arrangement?"

Curiosity gnawed at the edges of her restraint. She had never seen so many new faces inside the camp. Questions stacked up in her mind. Taking a deep breath, she reminded herself of what Renfield had taught her—information was shared on a need-to-know basis. That had always been hard for her to accept.

"Yes, they'll be with us for some time," Renfield replied. He offered no further details but smiled briefly before stepping away.

Revna turned from Ozias without another word—no goodbye, no polite dismissal—and disappeared into the crowd. Ozias stood watching, his arms folded across his broad chest, slightly amused by the silence. He was well aware that she was the only woman among the Bone Collectors, and her indifference piqued his interest.

Finding his fellow volunteers, Ozias took a seat as the combined council prepared to speak with the individuals selected to attend the meeting.

Renfield was acting quite odd when introducing her to Ozias, Revna thought as she disappeared into the crowd of semi-familiar faces. Ducking and dodging elbows and shoulders, she found a seat on a smoothly sanded bench near the dais where the council sat slightly elevated compared to those seated farther out. Naturally, she chose the side where her mentor sat—specifically in a place where she could read his face as words were shared with the collective.

Revna knew that words could hold empty meanings. It all depended on a person's level of facial control. Over the years, she'd learned the tells of the council members, especially those that indicated things were more serious than they let on—or when they were holding back important information.

Looking up just in time to see a stranger moving in to sit beside her, she pulled the belt that held her sword snug to her hips to keep the weapon out of the way. Nodding hello to the man, she was distracted by three loud taps against the wood of the dais.

"Can I get your attention, please!"

The voice boomed through the longhouse, deep and commanding. "Everyone, take a seat where you can. It is time to start this meeting called forth today by the council members of the Northern Bone Collectors and our guests from the West."

The man holding the silver halberd stepped back three paces to allow several older, silver- and white-haired men to step forward. The oldest of the six men moved to the center of the dais, raising his left hand into the air with fingers crossed. The soft whispering in the back of the room came to a halt. Holding his fingers up a moment longer, his raspy voice finally broke the silence.

"Collectors! We—" He dropped his hand and gestured to his colleagues. "—have called you, whom we've selected carefully, to hear about what the Northern and Western Bone Collectors have been working on."

He paused to cough. A young man brought him a carved bone cup filled with water. Taking a drink, he stepped back, and a salt-and-pepper-haired council member stepped in.

"We've been gathering intelligence on a large group of beasts traveling across the continent, leaving destruction in their wake."

As he described the therianthropes causing havoc, Revna leaned forward on the bench. Her dark gray eyes locked onto the council's faces. These were Bone Collectors from both the North and West—the best hunters and trackers from either side. It hadn't even occurred to her that she was among the greatest. Focused entirely on reading the expressions of the council, she looked up during a moment of pause and caught Ozias staring at her.

He didn't look away. His piercing eyes held hers, and a smile formed on his lips before he turned his attention to the next speaker. Glaring briefly at him, Revna turned her attention back to the familiar voice of Renfield.

"We Bone Collectors of the North have paired many of you with counterparts from the West. You're to get them familiar with the land and go on missions together."

Meeting her mentor's gaze, she saw the smile in his eyes. "What are you planning?" she muttered just loud enough for the man beside her to possibly hear. He gave no indication he had.

Feeling her shoulders tighten, Revna braced for what

was coming.

"The idea is to intercept the therianthropes as they break into hunting parties—whittle down their numbers. Pick off the weak. Strike when they least expect it."

Renfield's strategies were infamous, and his kill count unmatched. The executioner was known for more than just leadership.

The announcements continued before concluding with the Northern Collectors lining up to receive their partner assignments from the West.

Revna stood mid-line, shuffling forward when prompted. Meeting Renfield's eyes, she let out a breath she hadn't realized she was holding. He was the only council member she allowed herself to relax around—something the others thought should be beaten out of her, especially since she was a woman. Dramatically letting her head hang before she could speak, a hand gripped her shoulder.

"Revna. Before you say anything, you will take this assignment seriously and be civil."

Ozias stepped up to her left. Her head lifted at the sight of his worn boots. "Hello, partner!" he said before she could speak.

Why did men always get the first word?

Tension returned to her shoulders as she forced a smile. "Hello, Ozias. I see we are to be partners for the duration of this joint mission."

He smiled, hands on his hips, elbows out. "I don't have to like this," she added under her breath, "but I will follow my orders."

Glaring, she turned and walked away from Renfield

without waiting.

She didn't check to see if Ozias followed. It didn't matter. Her legs carried her through the camp and out the gate. It wasn't anger exactly—it was frustration. Her first mission with male recruits had taught her to avoid working with men unless absolutely required. This was one of those situations.

"Men are so incompetent. I can't believe he wants me to partner up. I can track and kill alone."

Pacing, speaking louder than she realized, she didn't notice Ozias leaning against a gate post until he cleared his throat loudly. Arms crossed, he watched her with faint amusement. "Don't let me interrupt. This seems important."

She froze. Heat flushed her face. Seeing the small bag at his feet, her stomach sank.

"What are you doing with that bag?"

She didn't care that he'd heard her talking to herself. What mattered was that the bag meant they were to share quarters.

Marching up to him, she stabbed a finger into his chest. Ozias dropped his hands in mock surrender.

"Some ground rules! Don't try any funny business. Not with me, not with any villagers."

He backed up around the post with each jab of her finger, smirking. "Yes, ma'am!"

Taking a step back and giving her some space, he lifted his hand in the Bone Collectors' salute. Revna rolled her eyes and turned away.

With sarcasm set aside, Ozias grabbed his bag and hurried after his new partner.

The first night spent with a man in her hut had her on edge. She didn't sleep much, and every little sound had her eyes open. Each time she awoke, she immediately looked over to see the man she was forced to take under her wing sleeping soundly. His breathing was deep and steady.

Revna had moved her sword from the post near the table—where she normally kept it clean and sharp—to beneath her bed, within reach if Ozias made any movement she didn't approve of. Renfield had warned her about men and their "desires," and how important it was for her to live outside of camp. Maybe he'd freaked her out a bit, but she took everything he said to heart in order to keep herself safe.

Awake and sitting up on her already-made bed, she had dressed long before Ozias stirred. With her legs crossed, she practiced her breathing, meditating until her new partner opened his eyes. She heard Ozias stir in his cot. Opening her eyes, she met his gaze across the small room of the hut.

A long yawn escaped him, and he stretched out, one arm smacking into the wall of the hut. He quickly pulled it back and sat up on the edge of his cot.

"Awake already? I guess I expect no less from the great Bloodhound herself."

He used the nickname some men gave her—often out of spite, a veiled way of calling her a bitch—but she didn't flinch.

"Do you know why they call me that?" she asked, her voice low.

Blinking and rubbing the sleep from his eyes, it was clear Ozias didn't know the full story. Yes, she was one of the best hunters, and her uncanny sense of smell had led to the nickname. But those who hated her twisted it into something derogatory.

"You can sniff out your prey while tracking?" he offered, phrasing it as a question. He stretched again, more carefully this time.

"The men who despise the fact I'm female use it to call me a bitch," she said flatly. "The ones who use it with honor do so because I can pick up scents no one else can."

She closed her eyes and let the silence hang for a moment. Then she waved her hand toward her nose. "I can smell the bread cooling three roads up from here."

Ozias sniffed the air but caught nothing. With the direction of the wind, it was nearly impossible for him to detect anything. Unsure whether to believe her, he stood and reached for his shirt to cover his bare chest.

"Well, regardless of how you got your nickname, it's incredible what you've done. Word of your accomplishments traveled to our camp. I'm honored to work with you."

Revna said nothing as she watched Ozias gather his silver-inlaid battle axe and gear. She left her cot and moved to the front of the hut where her secondhand table and few chairs stood.

Ozias stood just outside the hut, watching the villagers bustle by—headed to market or tending morning chores. Though their tasks weren't all that different from those of the Bone Collectors, he still found them fascinating.

Stepping up behind him, Revna smiled. "Aren't they just wonderful? I find it peaceful here in Eyvindara. They've become a second family to me—after the Bone Collectors."

Ozias turned his head to meet her gaze, his eyes briefly falling on her smile before returning to the scene before them. His deep voice broke the silence.

"We must also be careful of those closest to us—especially with the threats we face daily as Bone Collectors."

A frown fell over his face as he turned fully to her. Renfield hadn't told Revna much about Ozias, but he had shared personal details about her with the man.

Unsure of what Ozias meant, Revna smiled and reached for the hilt of her blade—only to realize it wasn't resting at her waist as usual. A flush of heat crept up her cheeks. She turned quickly to retrieve her sword, remembering she'd taken it to bed the night before. A wave of embarrassment washed over her at her own caution.

When she returned, Ozias had secured his axe in the leather harness across his shoulders. Revna motioned for him to follow.

"Come. Let's get started. We have a lot to cover. First, I'll show you the land surrounding the village and the Bone Collectors' camp."

With that, they left the village and followed the path into the woods that connected the village to the Bone Collectors' camp.

For several weeks, Revna and Ozias ventured into the woods, traveling the trails and veering off-path. She challenged him with tracking local animals—efforts that often led to them bringing back meat to share. She taught him about the local flora: what was poisonous to touch, which plants were used in darts and poisons, and what fruits were safe to eat.

Ozias was often overwhelmed by the flood of information, but Revna didn't ease up. One day, she placed two plates in front of him—each with a salad made from local plants and fruits.

"Which one is safe to eat?" she asked, arms crossed.

Ozias blinked up at her. She'd been tough on him, but there were moments—rare ones—where she showed unexpected softness. He admired her dedication, and her kindness to the villagers had won a part of him over.

He studied the plates. The leaves, the colors of the fruit, how similar they looked. He picked up each plate to smell them. Then, glancing at his teacher, he pushed one plate away and pulled the other closer. Picking up a piece of orange-red fruit, he bit into it confidently.

Revna dropped her arms and let her face shift to worry. Ozias's expression faltered. Then she gave him a thumbs-up.

"You chose correctly. But what would you have done if you ate the wrong one?"

She shook her head and dumped the poison salad into a bin with a lid.

"We'll use this later."

Ozias grinned and finished the fruit from the safe plate. "I'd put my life in your hands and hope you'd save me."

Revna rolled her eyes and let out a laugh. "I may just let you go, so I can be free of my duties."

Gawking in mock offense, Ozias huffed. "You wouldn't dare. You're too honorable, Revna."

She laughed again, this time with him.

The time they had spent together gave them the ability to know one another better—so much that they learned each other's tells when it came to hunting and tracking. Moving in sync, they were beginning to be the talk of the camp. "One of the best hunting and tracking duos put together since the two Bone Collector camps came together," some were saying.

Ozias had come to Revna with that rumor one evening while she sat near the fire pit outside her hut, cooking some of the meat of a deer they had caught earlier that day.

Rolling her eyes, she said, "And when you leave, I will be the butt of all their jokes again. Ha!"

She let out a loud sarcastic laugh as she stood, turning the meat over the spit. She could feel Ozias looking at her.

"Oh, don't look at me like that."

Sighing, she turned to the man she had become so open and close to—maybe even felt something for, although she would never openly admit it.

"I may be one of the best trained in the camp, but it wasn't because I was taken under the wing of Renfield."

Pulling the deer meat from the fire, she stepped away to gather the utensils needed to carve the meat from the bone.

"I had to push myself beyond limits that only a woman has. Limits I was—and still am—mocked for having, although I have proven time and time again that I can hold my own."

Setting a large, roughly carved wood plate down near the meat still tied to the spit, Revna carefully took the knives she had carried over and started to carve thin slices of meat from the whole.

Ozias closed the space between them without a word. Kneeling behind Revna, he placed a calloused hand on her shoulder. Feeling her stiffen at his touch a moment before relaxing, Revna dropped the knives into the pile of meat on the plate and slowly leaned back into the arms of the man she had been working with all this time.

Taken by surprise, Ozias released her shoulder to catch her in his arms, embracing Revna from behind. Silence crept over the two of them—not quite awkward, but heavy.

Seconds passed like minutes. Revna tucked her feet underneath herself, then used her hands to push against the ground and stand.

"Please excuse me."

Heat threatened to take over her cheeks as she bent over to retrieve part of their evening meal, pausing a moment to regain her composure before disappearing into the hut.

Ozias stood from his crouch, his eyes falling to the slowly dying embers before him. Swallowing hard, it felt like his heart had pounded its way up into his throat. Was it butterflies he was feeling in his stomach? Or was he so hungry from the day's work he felt ill?

How could he have let his wall weaken so easily? His thoughts came one after another, as he fought off feelings he hadn't ever felt in his lifetime. His life had always been dedicated to the Bone Collectors—or so he thought. Would this be the one time, the one woman, who changed that?

Getting his head clear, Ozias decided it was time to join his partner for their dinner before retiring for the evening.

The sudden sound of a snapping branch pulled Ozias' attention back toward the cooking spit. A messenger on horseback stood nearby. The horse's tail swayed back and forth, harshly cracking at the flies that threatened its legs.

At the loud crack, Revna had left the hut with her sword drawn.

"Ozias!"

As she came out, Ozias threw an arm out to stop her in her tracks.

"No need to cut down the messenger, Revna."

Squinting her eyes, she lowered her sword, trying to see the man over the glowing remnants of the fire.

The man tugged on the reins to steady the horse before dismounting with a loud thud.

"Excuse my rudeness," the man said, looping the reins around a low-hanging branch of a nearby tree. "I am a messenger of the Bone Collectors. I come with a message."

Lowering her sword, Revna sheathed it at her side. Walking around Ozias' still-outstretched arm, her eyes stared down at the man before her.

"What message do you bring us?"

Ozias let his arm fall away, holding his position as Revna asked the questions.

The messenger was a young, slender man dressed in thick brown leathers, armed with a hunting knife at his left hip. Returning to the horse—dressed with a heavily worn saddle and bags on either side—the man flipped open the left flap. Without another glance at the two before him, he dug around until he found what he needed, pulling out a rolled-up letter sealed in black wax.

Ozias acted before either of the others could. Meeting the man two steps into his walk toward them, he casually reached for the sealed letter.

"Thank you for your services. Ride safe, brother."

Reaching out to tap the man on the shoulder, Ozias watched him nod and quickly return to his horse. Revna observed the fellow Collector mount up and ride away.

Ozias popped the black crossbone seal and carefully unfolded the parchment, his piercing blue eyes scanning line by line. When he finished, he handed it over to Revna without a word.

Eager to read, she took it without hesitation. Her eyes fell to the neatly written words.

The silence between them grew heavy. Finally, Revna rolled up the message.

"It appears that we have little time to prepare."

Ozias met her gray eyes. The look they shared spoke volumes that only they would understand—feelings only the two of them could pick up on. Anticipation filled the space between them—for their first mission together as partners, and as something more than friends.

Revna felt a heat rise on her cheeks as she held the look a moment too long for her preference. She turned around, crushing the letter in her hands.

"I am going to pack my bag and change into my hunting leathers."

She could still feel the burn on her cheekbones as she hurried into the hut to get her gear prepared for the road ahead. With very few hours before first light, she wanted to maximize her time. Was she just using her time wisely, or was she avoiding Ozias? They had been given their first mission after weeks—no, months. Pausing as she sat on her cot to slide her boots on, she thought about how long they had spent together training and hunting in the area around her territory.

Winding the laces of her boots one at a time, she pulled them tight, ending with a bow and tucking them into the tops. Looking up, she saw Ozias now in the hut, preparing his own gear.

"It truly has been months that we've spent together, hasn't it?"

Sitting on the thought a moment longer, she leaned forward, resting her forearms on her knees. In all that time, she knew something inside her had changed for the man who had once been quite insufferable. Revna had never had a taste for men, nor cared to look at them long, having been raised in a whole camp of dirty, rude men.

Ignoring the tingle in her chest and the tiny flutter in her stomach, she decided her nerves were up from the first mission with a stranger-turned-partner. History had shown her that anyone—partner, party, or otherwise—was unreliable.

Shaking her head as if to clear her thoughts, she stood and reached for the sword she always carried on her left hip. Securing the blade into place, she decided this mission warranted her father's silver-bladed spear.

Kneeling beside her cot, she rested on her knees with her hands on her thighs. Staring into the shadows under the bed, she saw old worn cloth wrapped around a long object. It wasn't just one cloth—it was a wolf pelt tied with leather twine.

While Revna seemed to be meditating, Ozias, now dressed and armed for the road, had prepared dried food and filled both their canteens with water.

The letter had come from the Bone Collectors' high council. Word had reached them from the outer villages: a feral pack of therianthropes had been sighted in the area. The pack had been attacking tradesmen and farmers who came to town to sell their goods. Revna and Ozias were tasked with tracking and eliminating the threat before it reached the villages.

Simple enough? A feral pack of what—three or four? It was guesswork until they could assess the situation.

Revna drew in a breath as she leaned forward and pulled the fur-wrapped spear from beneath her cot. She hesitated, then sat back with the bundle on her lap. Running her hands down both ends of the fur, she found the folded edge and peeled it back to reveal the weapon.

Ozias stepped silently behind her, observing what looked like a personal ritual. Picking up the spear in both hands, Revna stood, allowing the cloth to fall at her feet. Holding the spear upright with her left hand, she ran her right hand up the blade to test its sharpness. A nick caught her skin, and she pulled her hand back on reflex.

Turning, she found Ozias just a few feet behind her. Startled by his closeness, heat flushed across her cheeks.

"Ozias, I didn't hear you."

Feeling the burn in her face, she dug the spear's base into the floor. Looking past him at their packed supplies, she stepped around him. "Everything appears ready. I suggest you rest. We're leaving at dawn's first light."

Taking the spear, Revna sat at the table to sharpen the blade.

The next morning came faster than expected. Revna stood from her cot, stretched, then picked up her pack and slung it over her shoulder. Securing her weapons, she exited the hut to find Ozias ready.

"All right! Let's be on our way."

With her father's spear in hand, she led the way out of the place she called home—taking with her the first person in a long time she'd ever trusted with her life.

They traveled most of the day, taking the main roads through established villages and towns. As they approached the region where the feral therianthropes had been reported, Revna began to search for tracks. Every so often she would kneel, fingers tracing the ground where animal pads had pressed into the mud.

Some tracks belonged to wolves, others to prey animals.

Ozias followed behind her, scouting for anything unusual. Finally, she found what she was looking for. Her hand landed in a print much larger than any normal wolf's.

"Ozias, we have werewolves."

Standing with her spear in hand, she moved several feet, searching for more. Pushing through brush, they started to count the tracks.

"I'm counting at least three," Ozias said, adjusting the battle axe on his back.

"I think you're right. I'm not finding anything else—no sign of other werebeasts."

Looking up at the sky, Revna saw the colors shifting to orange and pink. The sun was setting. Deep in the woods with little clearing, they finally found a spot to set up camp. The stars were already high above them.

Revna's legs burned with the day's work. But with her dedication to the Bone Collectors, she had learned to ignore the pain. Ozias dug a small fire pit to mask the light from wandering eyes.

Revna sat down by the blaze and pulled her pack into her lap. Opening the flap, she took out some dried meat.

Ozias returned from gathering wood, watching her nibble carefully at the jerky.

"Why don't you get some rest? I'll take the first round."

Something about his tone made her feel like he was worried she was weak—as if she needed rest more than him. Trying to stifle that stubborn pride, she swallowed and replied, "Sure. Better for the strongest of us to take the last watch."

Grinning at him, she winked.

Ozias just shook his head with a wide smile and took up post at a tree near the fire. Revna placed her pack beneath her head and lay down to sleep.

Falling asleep came easily under the stars. She had learned to grow used to the sounds of the wild, thanks to Renfield. He had taught her that comfort was no longer a luxury. Being a Bone Collector meant being rough and unkempt.

In the distance, a howl pierced the sounds of the crickets and the owl perched in a tree yards away. The howl lingered in the air for a long moment, echoed by three others—each one a different pitch.

The fire had died out, and the sound of Ozias being

slammed against a tree woke Revna from a deep sleep.

"Revna!"

Blinking her eyes, Revna, slightly confused about where she was as she came from a dream of her past, realized their camp had been invaded by the feral werewolves they had been tracking. Throwing her left hand out, searching in the dirt for the handle of her spear, she scrambled to her feet to find Ozias rising, his battle ax in his hands.

A large black and gray werewolf came charging out of the shadows at Ozias with its maw wide open, claws tearing at the air for him. Dodging the incoming beast, Ozias managed to cleave his ax up into its chest cavity.

Coming in from the side, Revna stabbed the werewolf in the ribs with the silver-inlaid spear. As she pulled the blade free, Ozias struggled to clear his ax from the corpse. Another red-furred werebeast burst from the trees behind them.

Turning, Revna lifted the spear just in time to catch the beast in the gut. The weight of the werewolf dropped her to her knees. Her knuckles turned white as she struggled to hold the shaft steady, the wolf swiping its claws at her face while she pushed the blade deeper.

Another deep howl—this one filled with pain—echoed through the trees.

As Ozias finally freed his ax from the fallen wolf, a third werewolf clamped its jaws around his left shoulder. Feeling the teeth sink into his flesh, Ozias tensed with the realization of what had happened. Pulling himself free of the beast's jaws, he turned his blade upward and swung it through the creature's neck.

Revna had ended her struggle with the red-furred

werewolf and turned to assist Ozias, only to find him covered in blood.

"Ozias! Are you okay?"

Walking up behind him, she watched him turn to meet her eyes with his own piercing blue gaze.

"Revna."

He dropped his battle ax, letting the bloodied blade rest in the dirt.

"Don't come any closer."

Looking at him, confused, she finally noticed the blood pouring from the bite on his shoulder. The leather was torn, bits of his flesh missing.

Dropping her spear without a second thought, Revna stumbled toward him. "Oh no. Ozias... no..."

Tears welled in her eyes—something she hadn't felt since she was a young girl. A tightness grew in her chest. Her stomach turned. She felt sick. Her breath caught in her throat.

Confliction overtook her—pain in her chest. What to do? She knew what she was taught. She knew what Bone Collectors did.

"Revna. You must do it." She heard the pain in his voice. He knew the rules. "You must kill me."

She shook her head, unable to stop herself. Walking up close, face-to-face, the tears began to fall. "I can't."

Unsheathing her sword for her, Ozias pressed the pommel into her hand. "Revna, you must do this. Do this for me."

Nodding, she leaned into him for a moment, her head resting against his bloodied chest. Clutching her sword in both hands, she kissed the man before her, the blade resting between them like a child.

Closing her eyes, she felt the blade slide up into his chest.

As the kiss between them weakened, Revna pulled the sword free and stepped back. Dropping the weapon, she reached out to Ozias as he fell to his knees.

The silver was already taking effect—proof the curse of lycanthropy had begun from the bite.

"I am so, so sorry."

Weeping, Revna held Ozias as he faded away.

An Interview with Alina Anthony

WHEN DID YOU START WRITING AND WHY?

I started writing when I was fifteen years old, it was something to do to entertain myself. I fell in love with the idea of creating characters, people who could do things I couldn't do. Live a life of adventure with others in worlds of great fantasy.

WHICH AUTHORS OR BOOKS OR MEDIA INFLUENCED YOU THE MOST AS A WRITER?

I read a lot of fantasy, I watch a lot of fantasy. I fell in love with Authors like Laurel K. Hamilton and Charlaine Harris, Anne Rice.

WHICH AUTHORS OR BOOKS OR MEDIA HAD THE BIGGEST IMPACT ON YOU AS A PERSON?

I don't have a major author that had an impact on me as a person, but reading Brom Stoker's Dracula led me through the gateway to other fantasy.

WHICH OF YOUR ORIGINAL TWELVE EMERGE STORIES ARE YOU MOST PLEASED WITH?
Moonlight Fears and Silver Tears.

WHICH OF YOUR ORIGINAL TWELVE EMERGE STORIES DID YOU FIND THE MOST DIFFICULT TO WRITE?
Golden Rods and Griffins.

WHAT BOOK ON WRITING DO YOU RECOMMEND?
I have never used a book on writing, or read a book on writing. I have taken a lot of writing classes, even some courses from community colleges for fun.

WHAT ADVICE WOULD YOU GIVE AN UNPUBLISHED WRITER?
Never give up on your dream to publish a book, keep writing and reading. Adopt what you love from other authors, everyone has a piece that can be learned from them.

DO YOU HAVE A "DREAM PROJECT" AS A WRITER? WHAT WOULD IT BE?
I have a novel I would love to write with a friend, a novel with two of our characters we have been carefully developing in a world with werewolves and elves.

Your stories will be published in a set of *Prompt* collections with the other Third Generation authors but also as a collection of just your own work. Did you have a conscious theme for your personal collection?
I did not have a conscious theme, I used every prompt to help extend my writing style. To challenge me as a writer and to bring out ideas I wouldn't have thought of before.

Who do you write for and how does it drive you to create?
I write for myself really, but I've shared some of it with others. I've co-written stories with many other people, but always kept it a secret from my family afraid they would think I was bad or embarrass me. I have now started sharing my works and have found overwhelmingly positive feedback.

Optimally, we're always growing and improving as authors. Talk about how you grew or changed as a writer over the course of creating your stories for *Prompt: The Third Generation.*
I have found I can write more than what I am used to, I've found inspiration from my own experiences in creating my stories. Having a timeline to get my stories done was a great challenge for me, getting started was always hard. It was a great growth for me, showed me I could do something like this under great pressure.

IMAGINE THE PERFECT COVER FOR YOUR PERSONAL COLLECTION. DESCRIBE IT... EVEN IF IT'S IMPOSSIBLE.
A ten year old girl with dark hair standing in a field of grass under two moons, looking off into the distance holding a spear of silver. She is dressed in a white dress with boots of fur, with a wolf howling in the distance.

Alina Anthony is a fiction writer that hails from Nebraska, making her debut with this showcase collection. A love of living in other worlds and of fantasy has given her the opportunity to write many stories. Alina believes in nurturing the imagination, and holding on to her inner child forevermore. Writing has always been a gateway for self-healing for her, and a way to cultivate friendships with other authors and readers alike.